Shakespeare
and
LEGS

NORA MCLINTOCK

Cover by Brian Boyd

D0040742

Scholastic-TAB Publications Ltd.

Scholastic-TAB Publications Ltd.
123 Newkirk Road, Richmond Hill, Ontario, Canada L4C 3G5
Scholastic Inc.
730 Broadway, New York, NY 10003, USA
Ashton Scholastic Pty Limited
PO Box 579, Gosford, NSW 2250, Australia
Ashton Scholastic Limited
165 Marua Road, Panmure, Auckland 6, New Zealand
Scholastic Publications Ltd.
10 Earlham Street, London, WC2H 9LN, UK

Canadian Cataloguing in Publication Data

McClintock, Norah.
Shakespeare and Legs

ISBN 0-590-71777-4
I. Title.

PS8575.L56S48 1987   jC813'.54   C87-093614-X
PZ7.M24Sh 1987

6 5 4 3 2 1   Printed in Canada   7 8 9/8

Manufactured by Webcom Limited

Chapter 1

Elise cupped her bare hands in front of her mouth and blew on them to warm them. Then she rubbed them quickly together, hoping that a little friction would take the numbness out of her fingertips. Before bending down to tighten the lace on her right skate, she stared out across the snow-covered expanse of the frozen bay.

Ordinarily she loved the frigid months of the year when the St. Lawrence was frozen and she and the rest of the kids in town could put on their skates and glide forever along the shoreline. Ahead and to her right a dozen younger boys had cleared the thick layer of freshly-fallen snow from a large rectangle of ice and, using their shovels for goal posts, had begun an energetic game of hockey.

Elise barely noticed them, despite the enthusiastic shouts peppered with swear words that accompanied their game. Her eyes were fixed far beyond them, off to the west where a point of land jutted out into the bay and blocked the old village of Ste-Marie from view.

She watched a moment as two figures sailed hand in hand towards the very tip of the point.

Then she bent once more to her skates.

Starting at the bottom, she pulled the lace tight at each hole until the skate supported her ankle firmly. As she worked, she wondered why she'd even bothered to come. She wasn't wanted here. She shouldn't have jumped so quickly when Laura called. She should have known that the invitation was too good to be true.

But there she'd been, sitting up in her room after lunch with all of Sunday afternoon yawning before her like some great dark pit into which she was doomed to topple, when the phone had rung. She had heard it out in the hallway but hadn't made the effort to heave herself off the bed to answer it. It wouldn't be for her. It was never for her these days.

Then her mother's voice had called from downstairs, summoning her, and when Elise had picked up the upstairs extension and said a tentative, curious hello, it had been Laura's voice on the other end.

"Let's go skating this afternoon."

Elise had been so startled by the invitation, so pleasantly surprised, that it hadn't occurred to her to ask if they would be going alone, just the two of them, the way it had always been in the past. She had simply and delightedly said yes, and it wasn't until the doorbell rang and she'd flung the door open to find Laura and Antoine standing on the porch that she'd understood that this was not one of the good old days.

If Laura and Antoine had simply dropped by on their way to the bay, Elise would have found some excuse not to go with them. Instead, answering the door with her coat already on and her long black scarf already wound half a dozen times around her neck, she was trapped. She could think of no way out. She slung her skates — tied together by their laces — over her shoulder and shut the front door behind her.

Elise lived at the foot of Hillcrest Avenue, which ran right into Lakeside Drive. Walking to one side of Laura, with Antoine on the other side holding Laura's hand, Elise trudged unenthusiastically through the snow towards the bay. The threesome eventually crossed Lakeside Drive and climbed down a steep flight of stairs to what in the summertime was a mooring area for pleasure boats. Now, in the depths of February, the docks had long since been pulled out of the water and the vast bay stretched clear and downy white as far as the eye could see to where the snow-covered surface of the lake blended into pale, greyish clouds at the horizon.

They found a log that had been caught in the freeze and was now embedded in the ice, and sat down on it to change from boots to skates. Elise worked quietly while she listened to Laura chatter on about skating down to the village and stopping at Étienne's for hot chocolate. Étienne's was a tiny restaurant next to the grocery store opposite the village fire station. It was the one place open on Sunday afternoons — and that was only because the bus stopped there. Étienne was a ticket agent for the bus line.

"Be sensible, Laura," Antoine said as he stuffed

his boots into a plastic bag and tied it shut. He set the bag onto the snow beside the log, confident that it would be there when he had finished skating. For as long as Elise had been skating on the bay, she had never known a single pair of boots to disappear.

"How can we walk into the village on our skates? We'll ruin the blades." Although he attended the École Sécondaire St. Louis, the French Catholic high school, Antoine Laurier spoke flawless English without the slightest trace of an accent. Laura said this was because Antoine had been brought up bilingually. His mother was English speaking, his father a Francophone.

"We'll take our boots with us," Laura said brightly. "Then we can change them when we get there and walk up for some hot chocolate. Once we're good and warmed up, we can skate back home again."

"Once I'm all warmed up, I don't want to have to freeze my butt off again," Antoine said with annoyance. "First we skate, then we warm up. Besides, it'll be dark by then. It's not safe to skate out here in the dark."

Laura's mouth sagged into a pout. She turned and fixed Elise with her wide, emerald eyes. Once again Elise was struck by the extraordinary thinness of the face, and of the beauty that had emerged with the loss of all those kilos. Like the first thaw of spring when the snow melts and one can see the beginning of a warm and beautiful summer, the determined dieting

Laura had undertaken had revealed a truly lovely young woman beneath the soft and heavy excess flesh that had plagued her from childhood. Elise still hadn't gotten used to this new, slim friend who seemed so often now to be almost a stranger.

"What do you think, Elise?" Laura was asking. "Want to skate down to the village for some hot chocolate?"

Elise looked at Antoine's shaking head and listened to his angry little clicks of disapproval and said, "Sure. That sounds like fun."

"It's a ridiculous idea," said Antoine. "Besides, it's too cold to make the trip all the way there and back." He stood up, leaving his boots lying in their bag next to the log. "If you want to go, be my guest, but count me out."

He pushed off with his left foot and began to slide across the ice away from the two girls. As he sailed away, Laura stuck out her tongue at him.

"He's so stubborn," she complained. "He always has to have everything his own way. He always gets into a real snit if things aren't done exactly the way he wants."

Elise watched Antoine's back as he stooped into a speed-skating position, the strength in his legs propelling him swiftly forward, away from them.

"If you want to skate down to the village," she said slowly to Laura, "I'll go with you and keep you company."

Laura's pouting lips curled upwards into a

grateful smile. "I knew I could count on you," she said. "I always can." She gazed out across the ice at Antoine. Elise quickly finished putting on her skates and stood up, the bag holding her boots in her hand.

"So come on," she said excitedly to Laura. "Let's go."

Laura sighed and shook her head. "I can't."

"But you just said..."

"If I go, Antoine will be furious," Laura said. "He probably won't talk to me for a week."

So? Elise wanted to say. Who'd even want to talk to a fifteen-year-old boy who acted like such a baby over something so trivial? But she held her tongue, sensing that she wouldn't get very far if she began to criticize Antoine. It was one thing for Laura to complain about his periodic moodiness — but let anyone else make a similar observation about him and she would immediately fly into a rage, saying that no one knew Antoine as well as she did and that therefore no one could presume to point out his faults.

Elise knew this from bitter experience. Once, soon after Laura had met Antoine, Elise had spent an entire afternoon at Laura's house while Laura waited for the phone to ring, instead of going to the movies as planned.

"He promised he'd phone me at noon," Laura had said when it was already twelve-thirty. "Let's just wait a few more minutes, okay?" When one o'clock rolled by, Laura was cursing Antoine and his thoughtlessness.

By two o'clock, Elise was annoyed too. "He's so

inconsiderate," she'd commented. "He's made us miss the movie."

Laura had reacted so angrily to Elise's comment that in the end Elise had apologized for the sake of peace, even though what she'd said had been mild compared to what Laura had been saying herself about him.

Elise let her boot bag fall to the ice. There was no point in arguing, so instead she just pushed off on the ice. Laura came behind her. In silence the girls followed the two-bladed trail left by Antoine until they finally caught up with him far out in the bay. Laura slipped one hand into his and the two of them remained together for the rest of the afternoon. All that Elise could do was skate a little off to one side, or trail behind them slightly. They seemed to have eyes only for each other, though Laura did make sporadic attempts to include Elise in what little conversation there was. Antoine steadfastly ignored her.

He probably regards me as a third wheel, Elise thought angrily. And that was exactly what she felt like, a useless, unnecessary and unwanted appendage to the self-contained and contented world of Laura and Antoine.

Gradually Elise let herself fall further and further behind. When Laura finally noticed Elise's absence, the distance that separated them had become so great that she had to shout at the top of her lungs to get Elise's attention.

"Aren't you coming?" she called.

Elise shook her head and pointed with exaggerated gestures to her skates.

"I'm going back to tighten them," she shouted. "I'll catch up with you."

Laura nodded and, turning away from Elise, skated on, her leather-gloved hand still securely encased in Antoine's. Elise skated alone, back to the log to tighten her laces.

When Elise's skates were so tight they practically stopped the circulation to her feet, she put her mittens back on and stood and looked way down the shore to the two tiny figures standing against the clear, clean white of the point. As she watched she saw Laura wave one arm slowly back and forth, high in the air. She wants me to hurry, Elise thought. Hurry and what? Tag along like a kid sister on a heavy date? She glided forward tentatively, then stopped. The wave could just as easily have been a goodbye wave, a see-you-later wave, an I'm-going-off-with-Antoine-alone wave.

Elise allowed herself to come slowly to a stop, then turned back to the log and sat down once more, this time to remove her skates.

As she thrust her stockinged feet into her frigid boots Elise glanced again down the shoreline. They were still there, silhouetted against the snow-covered banks of the point, Laura waving again. Elise stood up, slung her skates over her shoulder and turned back to shore.

As she trudged past the boys playing hockey, she imagined Laura watching her, then skating back as fast as she could to see what was the matter, to beg her to come along — the old Laura, the inseparable friend, the Laura who had pledged to be her friend for life and who had forgotten that pledge after a date with the first boy who had ever noticed she was alive.

Maybe she was coming after her, maybe by the time Elise reached land she would hear Laura's voice, strong and clear, calling to her to stop being so silly and come along.

But all she heard as her feet trod silently through the lush white carpet of snow were the hoots and screams of the hockey players. I'm not going to look back, she told herself. I'm not going to let on that I even care. I'm just going to climb those stairs and walk home. But when she reached the base of the wooden steps she couldn't stop herself. She turned slowly to see how Laura was reacting.

She scanned the length of the point and saw no one. Quickly her eyes shifted to the frozen wasteland beyond the tip of the point. Nothing. Laura was nowhere to be seen. Eyes stinging, cheeks burning in the cold of the waning afternoon, Elise began to stumble up the snow-covered stairs. She was gone. Just like that, Laura was gone.

Slowly she crossed Lakeside Drive and tramped along the sidewalk, staring down at her feet, not wanting anyone to see the tears gathering in the corners of her eyes. Not that there was anyone to see. It was far too cold for people to be lounging around idly out of doors.

"Elise!"

Startled, Elise's head jerked up and spun around as she tried to determine who'd spoken to her.

"Hey, Chessman. Over here!"

She looked to her right, into the Elliotts' front yard, and saw Bobby Elliott there, a big grin on his face. She'd known the Elliotts all her life; their backyard adjoined her own. And she had disliked Bobby Elliott for as long as she'd known him. He was an unpleasant boy who told nasty jokes and never, as far as she was aware, had a good word to say about anyone other than himself. Still, to be polite, she nodded at him and murmured a hello.

"Come over here a sec," Bobby said. "I need your help with something."

Elise held back, staying on the sidewalk outside the picket fence that marked the Elliotts' front lawn. Bobby was up to something. He was *always* up to something.

"Come on," Bobby said impatiently. "I'm not going to bite, for Pete's sake. I just want to ask you something."

Still she hesitated.

"Chessman..."

"If this is one of your stupid jokes, Bobby, I'm not interested," Elise warned him, taking a step closer.

Bobby held one hand up in the air. "Scout's honour," he said. "I just need some information, that's all."

Elise sighed as she crossed into the Elliott yard. "What kind of information?" she demanded.

"Come over to the porch a minute."

"What for?"

Bobby gave her a sour look. "What's the matter with you?" he asked. "Don't you trust me?"

"No," Elise said emphatically.

Bobby shook his head slowly and sighed."Look, if you don't want to be neighbourly..."

"I'm freezing cold, Bobby. I've been skating and

I'm on my way home. So whatever it is, hurry up, okay?"

He shrugged affably. "No problem," he said. "Step over here a sec and let me show you something."

Cautiously Elise followed him to the porch. Sitting on a small white wrought iron table was a box. Nestled in the box was a model airplane and a remote control unit.

"Nice," said Elise as she looked it over.

"Nice?" Bobby snorted. "Is that all you can say? Nice? For your information, I probably paid more for that little item than you make in a year's babysitting. It's the most sophisticated model airplane available. Top of the line. State of the art. A real collector's item."

Elise looked again at the model, then at Bobby. "And you're going to fly it on a day like this?"

Bobby beamed. "That's what I want to talk to you about," he said.

When Elise opened her mouth to protest that she knew nothing about model airplanes, Bobby waved her silent. "This baby is built to withstand anything," he said. "But still, a guy has to be careful. It's not every day you get your hands on a sleek piece of machinery like this."

"Would you mind getting to the point, Bobby?" Elise's teeth had begun to chatter. She couldn't wait to get home where it was warm.

"Okay, okay," said Bobby. "Keep your shirt on, will you? Like I said, this is a sturdy piece of machinery. But a guy's got to be careful. So what I wanted to ask you, Chessman, is this: What's the weather like up there above the cloud cover? I mean, is it turbu-

11

lent, or what?"

Elise felt her cheeks burn as if they'd been set aflame.

"Very funny," she snapped angrily. She should have known. He'd been teasing her about her height all her life. Bobby loved to torment anyone who was at all different, and to him Elise was a perfect target. He'd found many ways to do it — a thousand subtle approaches for his jabs. He had it down to a fine art — drawing Elise into conversation, teasing her the way an angler teases a trout with his lure, hooking her so slyly, so cagily that he could reel her almost all the way in before she realized she'd been hooked.

Elise was tall. Very tall. Over 185 centimetres in the flattest of heels. Easily the tallest girl in her entire school, probably the tallest girl in town, and quite possibly destined to become the tallest female in the whole country. The last couple of centimetres had been added in just the past month. Already she hated every centimetre of her being over and above the 165 mark, but it wasn't finished yet. Elise was still growing.

For as long as she could remember, Elise had yearned to be shorter. And for just as long, she had been tall, top of the height curve for her age group — the first girl that people noticed in any group.

"It's because you're so outstanding," her father used to joke, but she'd never found his humour funny.

"Don't worry," her mother said whenever Elise wished things could be different. "The boys will eventually catch up. You'll find someone taller than you soon enough."

As if being able to find a tall boy was the be-all and end-all of her troubles. Sure, it would be nice not to have boys shy away from her because she was so tall — taller than most of them — but that in itself wasn't really the problem.

The problem was that no one ever got a chance to find out if Elise was okay or not. Her height got in the way. It was like a wall around her soul, hiding from sight the fact that she was just an ordinary person.

Instead, Elise was the butt of an endless torrent of "tall" jokes, every one of which hurt her and pierced her heart. She would have done anything to be short and inconspicuous.

She turned her back on Bobby Elliott and his state-of-the-art model airplane and tried to block his laughter and taunting voice from her ears.

"Got you again, Chessman," he called after her. "You're as dumb as you are tall. I get you every time."

She forced herself not to run, even though she ached to stretch her long legs and sprint home as quickly as she could — away from Bobby and his teasing, away from Laura and her deceit, away from Antoine who had stolen Laura from her. But she didn't give in to the panic; she walked quickly but with dignity, head held high, tears burning her cheeks.

As long as her back was to Bobby, he couldn't see the tears. She continued down Lakeside, turned at Hillcrest, marched up the driveway of the first red brick house on the left and entered through the side door.

Straight ahead inside the door was a second door that led into the Chessman kitchen. To the left, a flight of stairs led down to the basement. Elise took the turn, went down the stairs and sat on a bench at the bottom to pull off her boots. She slid them under the bench and hung her coat on a peg on the wall. She hung her skates on a second peg, then headed back up the stairs and into the kitchen. Her mother was sipping a cup of tea while she read a paperback novel at the pine table. She glanced up at Elise when she entered.

"Have a nice time skating?" she asked brightly. Then, before Elise could answer, she added, "Your cheeks are as red as two apples. That's good. Growing girls like you need plenty of exercise and fresh air."

Elise winced at the word "growing."

"What's for supper?" she asked.

Besides being tall, she was as thin as a rake — and flat as a board too. And while three-quarters of the girls at school were constantly on diets, trying to lose a little here or a little there, Elise never seemed to be able to eat enough. No matter how she stuffed herself with sandwiches, cookies, fruit and ice cream, she never seemed to fill out.

"You should be glad," her mother liked to remind her. "The other girls would give their right arm to be like you."

It wasn't true, of course, but Elise said nothing. Most of the other girls were only too glad not to be as tall as Elise. Most of the other girls had bosoms. Most of the other girls had boyfriends. Even Laura.

14

Her mother sighed. "Your father won't be back from his symposium until late," she said, "so I thought we'd just have pizza for supper."

"Pizza?" Elise echoed in dismay. "It's Sunday! Most people have roast beef or roast chicken for Sunday dinner — with gravy on their potatoes and pie for dessert."

"Most people's mothers haven't spent the last three weeks devising, concocting and testing one hundred and one ways to dress up lamb," her mother said drily. "This is the first day in a month that I haven't had to go near an oven — and I plan to keep it that way."

Elise's mother was the food editor for a women's magazine. Every month she had to come up with two sets of recipes. The first emphasized what she called "gourmet cooking for the masses — easy-to-follow recipes from around the world."

The second set was geared to those on limited budgets. It included things like "winning ways with cream of mushroom soup" and "how to cook hamburger so they won't know it's hamburger."

And while Elise could understand her mother's lack of enthusiasm for cooking at home, given the way she spent her work week, still, it didn't seem right that the food editor of one of the biggest magazines in the country was about to stuff her own daughter with junk food.

"For heaven's sake, Elise," her mother said testily, "don't look so sullen. I'm not cooking and that's that. Let's just pretend we're Italian for the evening, okay?"

"Okay," Elise agreed reluctantly. "But I bet even

Italians don't eat pizza for their Sunday dinner."

"So while were pretending we're Italian, let's pretend as well that this is Tuesday," her mother said breezily. "I'm sure lots of Italian families eat pizza on Tuesdays."

It was supposed to be a joke, but Elise didn't feel like laughing. Instead she nodded sulkily, picked an apple out of the fruit bowl on the table and climbed the stairs to the second floor.

Her room was in the back, separated from her parents' bedroom by an enormous study used by both of them for work at home. One end of the study was stuffed with economics texts, her father was an economics professor at the university. The other end was crammed with cookbooks of every description.

Elise's room was bright and airy, facing south and catching most of the winter sun. It was painted daffodil yellow, which further enhanced its gaiety. The bedspread and matching curtains were a bright floral print, reminding Elise of a spring garden. But today the cheerfulness of the room did nothing to raise her spirits. Holding the apple still intact in her hand, she crossed to the window and pulled one of the curtains back to peer out across the long snow-covered yard, across Lakeside Drive, down to the lake. She could see the boys as small as ants in the distance, cheerfully chasing their puck. But the ice around and beyond them was still — silent and empty.

Chapter 2

Elise pulled the front door shut and checked to make sure it was locked. Both her parents left for work almost an hour before she had to leave for school. Both worked downtown, so both had to fight rush-hour traffic to get there.

Automatically, Elise headed down Lakeside Drive towards Laura's house. She was halfway there before it occurred to her that she didn't really want to walk with Laura this morning, not after the way Laura had treated her the day before. But she didn't change course. She couldn't. She'd been walking to school with Laura every day since they'd met in the second grade.

The only exception had been when one or the other of them was sick. Even in the past three months — since Laura had become friends with Antoine — the two girls walked together up to the highway and over the bridge to Paul Campbell High at the top of the hill.

The school was right across the road from a new nursing home. Elise wondered how the elderly residents were supposed to rest when they were subjected to the noise of eight hundred teenagers several times a day. She supposed, though, that the evenings were quiet enough. Antoine lived in an apartment complex north of Paul Campbell High and attended St. Louis a few blocks from his home. He and Laura didn't usually see each other until after school, when Antoine would walk over to meet Laura.

If Elise didn't stop by and call on Laura the way she did every day, Laura would think something was wrong. Of course, something *was* wrong, but it was one thing to be angry with Laura and quite another thing to take the drastic step of not calling on her. That would have been tantamount to severing diplomatic relations!

Still, having to wade through the snow while listening to a twenty-five minute monologue on the virtues of Antoine Laurier was more than Elise thought she could stand, especially today. Laura hadn't even telephoned on Sunday evening to ask what had happened to her — to find out if she was all right. For all she knew, thought Elise, I could have been stricken with some horrible disease and gone home doubled over in agony. She should at least have called.

Still, Elise didn't turn back. She'd call for Laura. If their friendship was going to come to an end, it wasn't going to be because of anything she did, she was going to make certain of that. If and when things were over between them, it would be because of Laura's rudeness and lack of consideration — the blame would be squarely on Laura's shoulders and no one would be able to say Elise hadn't tried.

Besides, if she called on Laura, Laura would certainly say something about the mysterious way she'd disappeared the day before, and who knows, maybe she *would* tell her that she'd suddenly begun to feel just awful, that she'd been afraid she was going to faint, and that it had taken every bit of her strength to get herself safely home.

If Laura didn't offer an apology, that was exactly what she was going to do. If Laura didn't offer an apology, then Laura deserved to feel bad for the way she'd treated her. It would serve Laura right.

Yes, thought Elise, that's exactly what I'll do. I'll show her. By the time she marched up the front steps of Laura's house and boldly pressed the doorbell with one thumb, Elise even had the exact words worked out in her mind.

Laura didn't answer. Her mother, in a quilted pink floor-length robe cinched tightly around her waist, a mug of steaming coffee in one slender hand, did. She opened the inside oak door, but left the outer aluminum and glass door shut and spoke to Elise through it, her voice so muffled that Elise had to strain to understand her.

"She left half an hour ago," Mrs. Syms said, lifting the cup to her lips. "Honestly, it used to be I had to wrestle Laura out of bed every morning. Now that she's going with that boy she's up and out of the house before I can even pry an eye open myself."

She said the words "that boy" with obvious distaste, her full, soft lips turning down into a frown.

Elise nodded and stepped back from the door, expecting Mrs. Syms to go back inside. Instead, she stayed in the doorway, peering angrily out the frosted glass.

"What do you think of Antoine?" she demanded. "Is he to be trusted?"

The question caught Elise off guard. "I beg your pardon?" she managed to stutter after a moment.

"You know what I mean," Mrs. Syms said impatiently. "Is he one of those boys who's likely to get a girl into trouble?"

"I don't know," Elise said honestly. She'd never even considered the matter. All she knew about Antoine was that he was the kind of boy who'd steal a girl's best friend away. Mrs. Syms clucked in annoyance.

"You two were always thick as thieves," she added. Then she abruptly swung the oak door shut with a bang, leaving Elise speechless on the porch.

Elise turned slowly and descended the steps. So Laura had gone on ahead. So she'd have to walk to school alone after all. Elise told herself she didn't care. If that was the way Laura wanted it, then fine, that was the way it would be.

But it didn't feel fine. As Elise trudged over the densely packed snow, listening to it squeak beneath her feet in the chilled, dry air, she felt lonely and defenseless — almost as though she were naked.

There were twosomes and threesomes, even entire gangs of kids making their way slowly towards the school, but Elise made no effort to blend in. She didn't know any of the others well enough to approach them, and no one invited her into any of the groups.

That was the whole trouble with high school, Elise decided. It was all cliques and gangs. Everybody, it seemed, belonged to one group or another, and they were all so clannish that switching from one to another wasn't easy. You were judged by the company you kept.

For years now, Elise and Laura had been a group unto themselves. Everyone knew that. It was an accepted fact and no one would ever think to change it. Up until now, Elise hadn't minded. It had never occurred to her that the situation might change one day. Nor had it ever crossed her mind to cast her net of friendship a little wider so that if things did change she wouldn't end up totally alone.

Another trouble with high school was that everyone had set opinions about everyone else. You were universally assessed and labeled, and that was that. Everyone knew that Cynthia Anderson was the smartest kid in the whole school and that she liked to study. Everyone knew that Myra Treacher was small and ugly and not very bright, and as a result was always alone.

And everyone knew that Elise Chessman was tall and skinny, and that she hung around with Laura Syms who — until recently, anyway — had been short and fat. They used to look like Mutt and Jeff together, and *had* to be weird because the fact never seemed to bother them.

Yes, everyone shared a common image of everyone else. The trouble was, that common image was always inaccurate. It was just that — an image, an external.

No one knew what life must be like for Myra Treacher, who never went to school dances, who was always picked last for group projects in science lab, and who always ate her lunch alone at the back of the cafeteria, staring out into space.

Certainly no one seemed to know or care how tiresome tall jokes were to Elise or what she was really like in her soul, where it counted. They only saw her height, not the real Elise, and she hated that. She longed to get out of school and as far away from Ste-Marie as she could possibly go, to a place where no one knew her and she could start afresh with people willing to judge her differently. If, that is, they could get over being struck by how tall she was — how unlike them, how unfeminine, how gangly, how freakish her proportions. And those, Elise knew, were big ifs.

She walked on with her head down, staring at the ground beneath her feet, shrinking into herself. She didn't look up until after she'd passed the nursing home and was entering the schoolyard.

The moment she looked up, Elise saw Laura standing outside near the front doors. Antoine was with her and they were standing so close together that the vapour from their breath melded into one small cloud as they spoke.

Elise paused a moment, wondering what to say, wondering if she should mention that she'd been to Laura's house and had been disappointed to find her already gone. Antoine was bending down slightly. His lips brushed one of Laura's reddened cheeks. They probably wouldn't notice if the Queen of England went by in full parade, Elise thought as she continued walking. She could probably breeze right past without Laura even being aware of her passage.

She was not more than three paces away when Laura suddenly looked away from Antoine, her emerald eyes sparkling. Elise forced a smile as her eyes met Laura's.

"Oh, hi," Laura said perkily. "Guess Mom told you I'd gone on ahead, huh?"

Elise nodded. She'd been angry before. Now, confronted with what appeared to be a complete lack of contrition on Laura's part and with no sign of an apology for the inconvenience, she began to seethe.

"Are you going to stand out here all morning?" Elise asked in an acid tone of voice.

Laura glanced at Antoine and giggled. "No. I'll be along in a minute. Meet me at my locker, okay?"

Elise shrugged and turned away. She wasn't sure she'd go to Laura's locker. It would serve Laura right if she didn't.

She made her way down the crowded first floor corridor to her own locker in the west wing of the school and, after opening the combination lock, pulled off her boots and put them on the newspaper liner inside. She took her shoes off the top shelf and stepped into them after first hanging up her coat. Then she gathered her books for the morning classes and closed her locker again.

Elise decided to give Laura another chance to explain and apologize, and headed towards the newer east wing of the school where Laura's locker was located. If Laura at least did that much, then perhaps their friendship wasn't over. Perhaps there'd be a way to work through their difficulties.

But Laura wasn't at her locker. Elise glanced at

23

her watch. Another five minutes yet before the homeroom bell went. She leaned against the cold steel of the locker door and waited. Gradually the halls began to clear as students drifted into classrooms in plenty of time to answer the homeroom roll call, or to finish homework assignments — or just to catch up on the latest gossip. Elise peered impatiently up and down the corridor, her foot tapping on the tile beneath her feet.

If there was one thing Mr. Nyman, nicknamed the Weasel by his students because of his beady eyes and long pointy face, could not abide, it was tardiness. His method of punishing late students was feared by all.

When the bell finally rang, Elise jumped in surprise. She'd been so preoccupied with Laura that she hadn't considered the possibility that she herself might end up in the Weasel's bad books. She ran down the corridor towards the nearest flight of stairs. Mr. Nyman's classroom was on the second floor.

When she came to the hallway leading to the gymnasium, a quiet command stopped her in her tracks. Elise turned to face white-haired Mr. Ouimet, the principal. His permanent smile and soft-spoken manner only enhanced his air of authority. It was said that Mr. Ouimet's smile remained in place and his voice didn't change even when he was meting out such severe punishments as suspensions or expulsions. No one had ever seen him lose control. He kept his emotions so firmly in check that it was impossible to tell what he was really thinking at any given moment.

"Yes, Mr. Ouimet?" Elise asked in a trembling voice. Running in the hallways was strictly forbidden. And it certainly wouldn't escape his notice that she was also late for class.

Mr. Ouimet smiled pleasantly at her, as if he was about to comment on the brightness of the day. He rattled some loose change in his pocket. It was a well-known habit of his that frequently was compared with Madame Defarge's knitting while she watched heads roll from the guillotine during the French Revolution.

"You're late already," he smiled, still regarding her as benignly as an archbishop about to bestow a blessing, "so you might as well spare yourself further trouble by walking to class."

Elise cheeks reddened. She'd never been spoken to by the principal before. She stood awkwardly in the hallway, painfully aware that she surpassed his height by a good ten centimetres, and waited to see if she was to be punished for her transgression. But Mr. Ouimet merely jingled his coins and nodded pleasantly before turning and strolling away down the hall, peering through open doors into classrooms as he went, pausing a moment here and there to listen to what was being said.

Elise walked up the stairs and down the second floor hallway. The restraint she exercised was more taxing than an all-out sprint would've been. She was so nervous about walking into the Weasel's classroom while roll call was in progress that she could hardly keep herself from breaking into a gallop and risking whatever punishment would follow if Mr. Ouimet caught her again.

She reached Mr. Nyman's room six minutes after the bell had gone and stood in the hallway to one side of the open door, wondering how best to make her entrance. She'd seen kids arrive late before. Some strolled in as if nothing at all were amiss. Others crept in and tried to get to their seats before Mr. Nyman noticed.

No matter what approach was used, Mr. Nyman *always* noticed when one of his students was late. He usually made the hapless transgressor stand red-faced at the front of the classroom and endure a merciless grilling.

Elise bit her lower lip as she waited. Precious seconds ticked by. At last, she drew in a deep breath, held her head high and took a step towards the door. She'd decided on the straightforward approach, thinking that if she did her best to avoid looking like some sort of shameless criminal, perhaps he might not treat her as one.

She planned to walk into the room, walk straight over to Mr. Nyman's desk and apologize for being late. She'd be open about it. If she was lucky, Mr. Nyman would appreciate her forthrightness and, taking into consideration the fact that she'd never been late before, would let her off with a warning.

But the Weasel glanced up from his desk and spotted Elise before she'd even fully entered the room.

"Well, well," Mr. Nyman said in a tone that made Elise's shoulders slump in dread. "What have we here? If it isn't the late *Ms* Chessman."

He always addressed the girls in the class this

way. It was never "Miss," always "Ms," as if they were all feminists and he disliked them for it. Elise heard a few titters from the students.

"Well, Ms Chessman," Mr. Nyman continued, "do come in. Don't stand out there in the hall-way cowering."

Elise took a step forward, her cheeks scarlet now. She hadn't been cowering. But by saying that she had been, the Weasel was putting her at a disadvantage, making her out to be fearful when in fact she'd meant to bravely offer her explanation.

Elise was standing just inside the door now and was painfully aware that every eye in the room was fixed on her tall body. But she didn't dare look at any of her fellow students. Her eyes remained glued on Mr. Nyman. She couldn't have pulled them away if her life depended on it.

Elise opened her mouth. It felt like she'd breakfasted on wallpaper paste, so uncomforta-ble was the sensation.

"Mr. Nyman..." Her tremulous voice was a barely recognizable croak. The tremor made her sound more afraid than she really was.

Mr. Nyman smiled and turned to the class. "Some people," he said, "come into my class with a better-late-than-never attitude."

He paused and scanned the faces up and down the aisles. "However, let me tell you all now, such an attitude is not acceptable. Not acceptable at all.

"Tardiness is a manifestation of sloth, and sloth is one of the seven deadly sins. It is, therefore, not to be tolerated. The student — like Ms Chessman here — who is tardy, is the student who is not in control of life. The student who is tardy is inconsiderate of others, sloppy in personal habits and unworthy of respect.

"A person who cannot be on time is a person who will not go far in a world where time is money and where tardiness, in effect, constitutes theft against one's employers. What do you think the school board would do if I was to breeze in here ten or fifteen minutes late each morning?"

Mr. Nyman stood and faced Elise, studying her for a moment, his eyes running up and down her body.

"Suppose, Ms Chessman, that you tell the class why you were late."

Elise stared at the Weasel. She couldn't do that. Even if she could make herself speak in front of all those curious, unsympathetic faces after the humiliation she'd just been subjected to, she could never give the real reason why she was late — that it was all Laura's fault.

"We're waiting, Ms Chessman," Mr. Nyman said in a singsong voice. "And if you don't tell us now, then you'll stand in that exact same spot tomorrow morning and tell us then. If necessary, you will stand there every morning until you have offered both an explanation and an apology to the whole class for wasting so much of our time. Do you understand, Ms Chessman?"

Elise didn't doubt for a moment that the Weasel would do exactly what he said. She tried to run her tongue around the inside of her mouth, to moisten it so that she could find her voice, but even her tongue was heavy and sluggish. It seemed an alien creature that did not belong to her.

Mr. Nyman took a step closer to her.

Elise gulped. She opened her mouth. "I'm sorry, Mr. Nyman," she said in a voice so small that it sounded ridiculous coming from the lips of someone as tall as Elise. "I...I lost track of time this morning, sir. I'm sorry. It won't happen again."

Mr. Nyman said nothing. He stood before Elise, staring at her so intently that she was sure he was going to make her try again, expand on her reasons.

"Ms Chessman," he said at last, "you may take your seat. And if you are ever late again, you will be treated to a detention. Do you understand?"

Elise nodded mutely and wobbled down the centre aisle to her desk at the back. No sooner had she sunk onto her chair than the bell signalling the end of homeroom rang and everyone got up and headed for the door. When Elise reached it, she found Laura standing just outside, waiting for her. A great big grin illuminated her face.

"You looked terrified, standing up there," she said, giving Elise a poke in the ribs. "What did you think he was going to do, put you in front of a firing squad?"

Elise could feel the anger boiling up inside her. "It's not funny," she hissed. "It's your fault I was late, you know."

"My fault?" Laura exclaimed as they walked

quickly towards the girls' locker room. Gym was the first class of the day. "How do you figure it was my fault?"

"You asked me to wait for you at your locker."

Laura looked up in disbelief. "You're a big girl now, Elise — no pun intended. You can tell the time. I didn't make you late. I didn't tell you to stand by my locker all morning like a lost puppy. You did that yourself."

"What's that supposed to mean?" Elise demanded. " 'Like a lost puppy'?"

"Yesterday was another example, when you were sulking out on the ice instead of enjoying yourself with me and Antoine."

"Enjoying myself with you and Antoine? That's a joke! You two are so wrapped up in each other, I don't know why you even bothered to ask me along. And speaking of Antoine," Elise added quickly, not wanting to get too deeply into the subject right then, "you probably made him late for school as well. You're becoming irresponsible, Laura, you know that?"

Laura's green eyes blazed. She flicked her copper hair back over her shoulder. "And you're becoming really bitchy. You'd think it was all my fault that you don't have a boyfriend."

"What?" Elise's mouth gaped open in surprise.

"That's what this is all about, isn't it?" Laura demanded. "You've been angry with me ever since I started going out with Antoine. You're jealous."

They had reached the door of the locker room, but they hung back a moment, glaring at each other.

Before, Elise had been furious. Now her fury turned to humiliation as the truth of Laura's statement hit home. She felt a sudden pressure behind her eyes as the tears built up and threatened to spill down her face. Laura sighed and her face softened, when suddenly the door to the locker room swung open and Miss Graves the gym teacher stared out at both of them.

"You're late, girls," she said sternly. Then, when neither moved immediately, she added, "I didn't mean that as a compliment. If you two aren't changed and on the floor in two minutes flat, it'll mean laps. Five laps for every minute you're late. Get it?" And before either girl could answer, the door closed again.

"We'll talk later, okay?" Laura said. Now her voice was soothing, almost apologetic. Elise nodded glumly.

They had no chance to talk during gym class and after gym Elise was scheduled for Spanish class while Laura had French.

"See you at lunch?" Elise asked hopefully as they parted.

Laura shook her head. "Can't today," she said apologetically. "I'm meeting Antoine at lunch time. We're going down to the plaza for a bite."

"After school then?"

Laura shook her head again. "I'm sorry. I promised Antoine I'd go over to his sister's after school and help him baby-sit his nephew. But we will talk, I promise. We'll make time to talk."

Elise nodded unenthusiastically. "We're still on

for Friday, aren't we?" she asked. Friday night was the winter dance at school and, as they had since the days when they were freshmen, Elise and Laura had volunteered to handle the refreshments. It wasn't a job many kids wanted, since it meant missing the dance and spending the whole evening in the kitchen. But Elise and Laura had never minded. It was a pleasant enough way to spend a Friday night and by now they were so good at coordinating all the food donations and setting up the tables that their services were sought after as a matter of course. Besides, it was the only way they had of going to the dances. No one ever asked them for dates.

Laura nodded. "Of course we're still on," she said. "Antoine has to go out of town right after school on Friday. He's going to Ottawa for his grandmother's eightieth birthday celebration. This weekend I'm all yours."

Just like the old days, thought Elise. And the thought filled her with happiness.

Chapter 3

When the last bell of the day rang on Friday afternoon, twenty-seven copies of *MacBeth* slammed shut in unison in Mrs. Ingram's classroom. As the students rushed for the door, eager to begin their weekend, Mrs. Ingram called Elise over to her desk.

Elise approached the young English teacher without trepidation. She liked Mrs. Ingram and got along well with her. She'd had her for English for the past two years and regretted that she wouldn't have her the following year. Mrs. Ingram was expecting a baby in July and was planning to take at least a year off.

Smiling up at Elise, she said, "I hope you aren't too worried about tonight."

Elise shook her head. Mrs. Ingram was the teacher in charge of the refreshment committee. It'd been a long time since she'd had to do any real supervising. Elise and Laura knew exactly what they were doing.

"I think Laura and I have everything under control, Mrs. Ingram," Elise said, smiling in anticipation of the evening ahead with her friend.

Mrs. Ingram frowned while she absentmindedly patted her stomach. Although her pregnancy was in the early stages yet, she'd already taken to rubbing her tummy from time to time during the day — a habit that her students found amusing.

"But surely you know…" Mrs. Ingram said slowly. "You and Laura are such good friends…"

It was Elise's turn to frown. "Know what?" she asked.

Two tiny wrinkles appeared just over the bridge of Mrs. Ingram's nose as she muttered, "Oh, dear." But the lines vanished quickly and she began to smile again.

"Never mind, Elise," she said brightly. "It won't be a problem. I do have a replacement and although he's not experienced, I'm confident you'll show him the ropes and see that whatever needs to be done is done."

"I don't understand, Mrs. Ingram," Elise said. Something was wrong. Something was very wrong. An emptiness formed in the pit of her stomach.

Mrs. Ingram sighed. "Laura came to me on Tuesday, Elise. She told me she wouldn't be able to help out with the food after all and asked me if I thought I'd have much trouble finding a replacement. Well, naturally neither of you girls is easy to replace. You're both so good at the job. But what could I say? Laura has put in over two years service on the committee.

"I'm surprised she didn't tell you, Elise."

Elise felt totally betrayed. Tuesday. That was three days ago. The very day after Laura had assured Elise she'd help out in the kitchen as usual she'd gone to Mrs. Ingram and begged off.

It was bad enough to be lied to. But now, to have to hear the news from a third party...Elise felt her cheeks burning.

"She did mention something about it," Elise said at last. "I guess it must have slipped my mind."

Mrs. Ingram was peering up at her, trying to see beyond the mask of casual indifference that Elise was trying to effect. "Everything between you and Laura is all right, isn't it, Elise?"

Elise nodded and somehow even managed a smile. "Everything's fine."

"Are you sure? Because if there's anything that you'd like to talk to me about..."

Elise shook her head. "Everything's just fine," she said again. "And don't worry. The refreshments will be handled without a hitch, as usual."

Mrs. Ingram studied Elise's face a moment more before leaning back in her chair and nodding.

"I'm sure you're right, Elise," she said. "And good luck with your new helper."

As soon as she was in the hallway, Elise began to run towards Laura's locker. She didn't even care that Mr. Ouimet or one of the vice-principals might be patrolling the hall. All she could think about was that she had to talk to Laura, she had to find her before she left the school.

Laura wasn't at her locker. In fact, the whole new wing of the school was deserted, which wasn't unusual for a Friday afternoon. With shoulders slumped and head bent, fighting back tears, Elise trudged along corridors and hallways to her own locker in the old wing of the school.

At first, with her eyes focussed on the floor, she didn't see the figure standing in front of her locker. In fact, she was almost on top of Laura before she did notice her. Laura had on her boots and coat and was clutching a small pile of books to her chest.

"Where have you been?" she asked Elise. "I was beginning to think I'd missed you."

Elise reached for her lock and began to fumble with the combination. "I'm surprised you have the nerve to face me," she said acidly, spinning the tiny arrow towards the last of the three digits and yanking the lock open. She glowered down at Laura.

"You talked to Mrs. Ingram, right?" A flush began to stain Laura's cheeks. "Look, Elise, I can explain."

Elise put her copy of *MacBeth* on the top shelf of her locker. Then she kicked off her shoes and thumped them down on the shelf as well. She reached silently for her boots.

"Okay, you're mad at me," Laura said. "And I guess you have a right to be. But, look, Elise, what would you have done if you were me? I mean, I just found out that Antoine's grandmother's birthday party has been postponed. The old lady came down with the flu or something. So Antoine is going to be here all weekend and naturally he asked me to go to the dance with him tonight.

"Come on, Elise, how many times have I been to a dance at this school? And I'm not talking about hiding out in the kitchen all night either. I mean really dancing. Out there in the gym with the rest of the kids. With a guy. It's never happened to me before. You, if anyone, should know how I've prayed for the day to come when I could just thumb my nose at all those creeps who thought I'd never get a date.

"I mean, look at me. I'm not Ms Chubbo anymore. I'm thin. I've got great clothes. Guys actually notice me now. And I've got a boyfriend. Face it, Elise, if this was happening to you, you'd act the same way. You understand, don't you, Elise? You can see what this means to me."

Elise had tugged her boots on and now reached for her coat. She pulled it on slowly and silently.

"Come on, Elise, say something. It's just this once. I mean, what was I supposed to do? I just found out…"

"You found out three days ago," Elise said quietly. It took tremendous willpower for her to force herself to look Laura straight in the eye. As soon as she did, Laura's green eyes skipped away to stare at the locker next to Elise's.

"You knew for three whole days that you were going to the dance with Antoine and you didn't tell me. I had to find out from Mrs. Ingram."

"Okay," Laura said, her voice smaller now, her tone almost contrite. "Okay, I was wrong not to tell you as soon as I knew. But I was afraid to

37

hurt your feelings. I mean, lately you've become so sensitive…"

"So in order to spare my feelings, you decided not to tell me at all, is that it?" Elise made no attempt to keep the sting of sarcasm out of her voice.

"I was going to tell you," Laura complained.

"Oh, really? When? Tonight?"

"I was going to tell you right now. Why do you think I waited so long for you?"

"When you could've been strolling home arm in arm with Antoine? Thanks a lot, Laura! You're one terrific friend!"

Laura's body stiffened, as if she'd been physically assaulted by Elise.

"You're not exactly scoring top marks on the friendship scale yourself, you know," she snapped back. "A true friend would be happy for me that I've finally got a boyfriend. It's what I've always wanted. But instead of being happy for me, all you can do is gripe. That's not fair, Elise. It's just plain selfish. You get mad at me every time I see Antoine. If you had your way, I'd never see him at all. So don't try and give me that wounded victim routine. You know darned well you'd do the same thing if you were me."

Elise stared at her friend a moment or two. She felt as though she was facing a stranger, someone about whom she knew nothing. It used to be that she could second-guess Laura's every move. It used to be that if Laura started a thought, Elise could finish it. Not anymore. The old Laura would never have stabbed her so viciously in the back, would never have defended such behaviour.

"I would never treat a friend of mine the way you've been treating me lately," she said at last. "Friends don't act this way with each other."

"If you're saying that we're no longer friends, Elise Chessman," Laura said angrily, "well, that's fine with me."

With that, Laura turned abruptly and marched down the hall. The heels of her boots drilled into the floor tile and echoed loudly in the empty corridors. Even when she'd turned the corner and was out of sight Elise could hear her. Then she must have gone out the front door. A pall of silence fell over the school. Elise closed her locker door quietly, brushed a tear away from her eyes, and began to walk slowly towards the exit, hoping that Laura would be long gone by the time she reached it.

* * *

That evening Elise pulled on a new pair of black stirrup pants and a bulky black sweater and set off for school early to arrange the sandwiches and desserts brought in that morning by volunteers, and mix the punches. There were cups to set out on the serving counter, napkins for the sandwiches and cakes, and bags of ice to pack into the freezer.

When she arrived at school she had to ring the buzzer at the front door so that Mr. Litvak the janitor could let her in. It was early and he hadn't yet unlocked the doors for the dance. She followed him through the almost empty gym. Up at one end, on a raised platform, a disc jockey had set up his turntables and speakers and was sorting through his records, making sure he had his playlist in order. Mr. Litvak unlocked the door leading to the kitchen and stepped aside to let Elise pass.

"At eight o'clock I'll roll up the window," he said, referring to the metal screen that divided the kitchen from the gym. Elise thanked him, closed the door and began to check the bags of sandwiches she'd stacked in the fridge that morning.

It wasn't until a half hour had passed while she made up trays and covered them with plastic wrap that she began to wonder what had become of the assistant Mrs. Ingram had promised her.

When she'd finished with the sandwiches, she took a new green garbage bag, washed it out and set it in a pail so that she could mix the punch — ginger ale mixed with three different fruit juices.

Elise had just started to open the cans when the kitchen door flew open and a boy wearing a large fedora strode in.

"Kitchen's off limits. Get out of here," Elise announced crisply without looking up.

"I'd love to oblige," the boy said. "Unfortunately, I've been sentenced here for the duration. Mrs. Ingram was the presiding judge. And you, I take it, are the jailer."

The can opener stopped turning as Elise stood

and took a closer look at the boy.

The first thing she noticed was how handsome he was. He had pale blue eyes that sparkled as they regarded her and his nose was small and straight. His lips twitched at the corners with what seemed to be suppressed amusement. Beneath the felt fedora was a cascade of thick black curls.

"William Shakespeare Jones at your service," he said solemnly as he let his gaze wander, unabashed, from the top of her head to her toes. Then, as they stood facing each other, Elise noticed something else about her new helper.

He was short. A hundred and sixty-five centimetres, tops. She sighed. It figured. A guy that cute just had to be short. Not that it made any difference anyway — a guy that cute undoubtedly had a girlfriend already, if not half a dozen of them.

Grinning mischievously, William Shakespeare Jones craned his neck in an exaggerated fashion to look up at Elise's face again while she stood before him, embarrassed and tongue-tied, his survey over.

"Well, hel*lo* there, legs," he said with enthusiasm.

As if she'd been burned with a red-hot poker, Elise, snapped to attention. "The name's Elise," she said curtly. "Elise Chessman. *Not* legs."

The boy shrugged. "Elise," he said smoothly. "Nice name. And if you don't mind my saying so, nice legs too."

"Very funny," said Elise brusquely. She blushed

scarlet as she sat down again and bent over the juice cans.

William Shakespeare Jones perched himself on the edge of the table and watched Elise as she worked.

"So," he said, "what's a good-looking girl like you doing in the kitchen when you could be partaking of the magic of a high school dance? Fancy yourself a Cinderella, do you?"

"I beg your pardon?" Elise looked up at him sharply, expecting to see a face full of mockery. Certainly no one had ever before called her good-looking and maintained a straight face while doing it.

"How come you're not enjoying the dance yourself, instead of serving behind the scenes?"

"I could ask you the same question," Elise said as she finished opening the last of the cans. She leaned over and dragged the garbage bin closer to her work table, then began to pour juice into it. William Shakespeare Jones grabbed a can and began to pour with her.

"I'm being punished," he said breezily. "It seems that Mrs. Ingram is not a fan of *Mad* magazine. At least, she didn't appreciate my dramatization of the *Mad* version of *MacBeth*. Not in her classroom. She said she expected a more serious and scholarly approach to the bard from someone with a name like mine."

Elise reached for a second can of juice and upended it. "Is that really your name? William Shakespeare?"

The boy nodded. "It's a sick family tradition.

My dad's name is John Paul Jones. The original J.P.J. was the father of the American navy. What a joke, especially considering the fact that Dad grew up to become a hippie draft dodger. Came here during the Vietnam war and never went back. Dad's the eldest of three boys. Actually, as far as names go I guess he got the best of the bunch. His brothers are William Tell Jones and Robin Hood Jones. Seems once Grandpa got started he just couldn't kick the habit."

"Did your grandfather name you too?" Elise asked.

"Naw. Dad did that. Don't ask me why. Revenge, maybe. Only I'm smarter than my dad. Instead of wasting a lot of energy trying to keep my monniker a secret and turning twelve shades of red whenever someone finds out, like he does, I announce it right up front. You've got to admit, it's a name of distinction. My friends call me Shakespeare."

"Shakespeare?" Elise hadn't quite decided how seriously she ought to take all this.

"Yeah." He tossed an empty can of apple juice into the trash and said, "So, what's next? You're the boss, or so Mrs. Ingram says."

"There's a crate of ginger ale by the fridge," Elise said. "You could empty the bottles in here too."

He jumped off the table and bowed from the waist. "Your wish is my command, oh mistress," he said with a flourish of his hand.

As Shakespeare busied himself pouring the ginger ale into the bin, he said to Elise, "Hey, you

43

never did answer my question, legs. How come you aren't out there as the belle of the ball?"

Elise didn't answer, hoping that would be the end of it. But Shakespeare didn't give up easily. He repeated his question.

"Don't call me legs," Elise said testily.

Shakespeare's eyebrows rose dramatically.

"Touchy about our height, aren't we?" he said. "Frankly, I don't see why. I've always found that tall girls have a certain *je ne sais quoi.*"

"It's called visibility," Elise said irritatedly. "I'm usually head and shoulders above a low-hanging morning fog."

Shakespeare laughed. Elise shot him a dirty look. "Hey," he protested, "I was just being polite. I thought you were making a joke."

"If you were as tall as me, you'd know it was no joke."

Shakespeare shook his head and grinned. "You're barking up the wrong tree, legs. If I was as tall as you, well, I'd probably work more often."

"Work?" Elise frowned. What was he talking about?

"I'm an actor."

"Go on!"

"For real. I've done eleven commercials, usually portraying twelve-year-olds instead of the mature teenager I am. And two years ago I had a series out in B.C. Only lasted thirteen weeks, but it was great. I got an *ACTRA Award* for it. And I've also done a lot of theatre. With my terrific looks, I've always thought that if I could add another, say, twenty centimetres to my height, I'd be in the major leagues just like that." He snapped his fingers.

"You'll grow," Elise said with a sigh.

Shakespeare shook his head. "I don't think so. I'm already taller than my dad and two uncles. But, hey, don't get the wrong idea. I don't let it get me down. Alan Ladd was short. Paul Newman's a little guy. Al Pacino isn't a whole hell of a lot taller than me. Talent's the key and I'm loaded with that. One day I'm going to make it big."

He chuckled. "Get me *down*, get it?"

"Yeah, sure, I get it," Elise said sourly. "Like people are always asking me what I'm *high* on. People also keep telling me that I've already made it big," Elise added wryly, "if you know what I mean."

Shakespeare grinned. "Yeah," he said. "I think I'm beginning to get the big picture."

When Elise winced, he apologized. "Sorry. But *you* were kidding around."

"That's different."

"I guess. A bit like a mother saying, 'Lord, my kid is funny looking' — but let a stranger say the same thing and the fur will start to fly."

He spoke with such gusto and such familiarity — as if he'd known Elise all his life — that she couldn't help smiling.

He was a strange sort of guy, she thought. Certainly more interesting company than most of the other students she knew whom Mrs. Ingram could have drafted to help her.

45

As they mixed the punch and set out the sandwiches, Shakespeare kept up a steady stream of banter. Gradually Elise let go and stopped being on the defensive as she responded to his relaxed familiarity.

By the time the metal curtain was rolled up, the two of them had filled the two glass punch bowls and arranged the serving counter perfectly.

As people began to mill around, helping themselves to sandwiches and punch between dances, Elise realized how much she was enjoying herself. Then, around nine o'clock, she glanced casually over towards the entrance to the gym and saw Laura walk in, her arm entwined in Antoine's.

Laura had gone all out for her first appearance at a school dance. She had on a pale green dress that emphasized both her emerald eyes and her newly-slim figure. Her thick copper curls were swept up and held into place by rhinestone-studded combs. Make-up accentuated her already large eyes and her prominent cheekbones.

Laura looked beautiful. It made Elise envious to see that not only did Antoine keep his eyes glued adoringly to her, but most of the other boys cast appreciative glances at her as well. Even Shakespeare paused a moment to ask, "Who *is* that? Homecoming queen?"

"More like the swan princess," muttered Elise.

Shakespeare frowned. "What do you mean?"

"Never mind," said Elise as she retreated into

the kitchen, suddenly ashamed at having uttered such a thought aloud. She stayed as far away from the serving counter as she could for as long as she could so that she wouldn't have to face Laura. But finally Shakespeare called for another platter of sandwiches. Elise carried one over to him. As she did so, Laura approached the counter. She was smiling at some remark Antoine had made. When she saw Elise, her smile faded.

"Hello, Elise," she said stiffly.

Elise could feel her heart pounding. She stared at Laura a moment, then turned deliberately away without saying a word.

A few minutes later Shakespeare was beside her, empty punch bowl in hand. "Is there something going on between you and the swan princess?" he asked.

Elise glared at him. "That's none of your business!" she snapped.

He shrugged. "Suit yourself," he said. "I need a refill on this. And don't look now, but there's a swan approaching at nine o'clock."

Elise turned in the direction Shakespeare had indicated and saw Laura coming into the kitchen. Hastily she looked away, to concentrate instead on ladling the ruby-red punch from the garbage bag into the punch bowl.

But Laura was determined, and a moment later Elise couldn't help but be aware of Laura's presence.

"Look, Elise," Laura said in a conciliatory tone.

"About this afternoon...about what I said —"

"I don't want to hear a word from you, Laura Syms," Elise said stiffly.

"But I —"

"If my memory serves me correctly, this afternoon you informed me that our friendship had been terminated. That suits me just fine. So would you please leave the kitchen. It's off limits."

Laura stayed where she was. "Elise, I don't think you're being fair."

"Fair?" Elise couldn't believe that Laura had the nerve to even think of using that word. "You don't think I'm being fair? Well, that's a laugh after what you did to me. Get out of here, Laura!"

Still Laura held her ground. "No, Elise, I'm not going until you at least agree to talk this over calmly and rationally."

"Oh, yes?" asked Elise, her voice rising. "Well, talk this over rationally." And with that, she lifted the punch bowl high above her and tipped it's contents onto Laura's head.

Laura shrieked in surprise as the crimson liquid cascaded down over her, turning the delicate pale green gown into a soggy, red-streaked mess.

Elise was almost as surprised at what she'd done as Laura was. She let the punch bowl clatter to the tabletop and stared helplessly at Laura, watching while Laura wailed.

"I-I'm sorry, Laura," she said at last. "I-I didn't mean to —"

"Oh, yes you did," Laura screamed at her.

By now the commotion had drawn just about every student in the place. They crowded around the serving counter, staring at the unfolding drama.

Antoine had come into the kitchen itself, closely followed by Mr. Ouimet and Mr. Landers. Hot on their heels came Miss Everett. They all stared in stunned silence at Laura.

Then Mr. Ouimet stepped forward. With his usual placid smile only slightly askew, he calmly asked the damp and shivering Laura what had happened.

"She poured punch all over me," Laura wailed, pointing at Elise. Tears streamed down her cheeks. Elise wondered if Laura was playing up to the audience, but she soon realized she wasn't.

Laura had looked magnificent before her sudden dousing. This had been such a splendid night for her, and Elise had ruined it. The tears were no doubt genuine enough, but even so, Elise wasn't at all sure that she regretted her actions. As far as she was concerned, Laura had deserved it by treating her so shabbily.

Mr. Ouimet fixed Elise with his smiling glare, and to her surprise Elise didn't feel particularly afraid.

"Did you pour punch all over this unfortunate girl, Miss Chessman?" Mr. Ouimet asked.

"It was an accident," Elise said.

"An accident!" Laura's voice was so shrill and loud that it almost drowned out the music that still blared from the speakers in the gym. "She did it on purpose! It was no accident!"

Elise held herself straight and tall and looked down to meet Mr. Ouimet's piercing eyes.

"I was filling the punch bowl when she came in here and startled me," Elise said calmly. "She wasn't supposed to be in here. There's a sign clearly posted on the door saying the kitchen is off limits to everyone but the refreshment committee. If she'd paid attention to that sign, this never would have happened."

"She's lying," Laura sobbed.

Mr. Ouimet raised a hand for silence. Then he looked at Elise again, trying to assess the truth of her statement before speaking.

"Was there anyone else in the kitchen at the time of the, er, accident?"

"I was here," a voice answered from behind Elise. It was Shakespeare. She turned and looked impassively at him. Let him say what he wanted, she thought. She'd have no choice but to take whatever punishment came.

Mr. Ouimet turned to face Shakespeare. "And you are?"

"William Shakespeare Jones," Shakespeare said. "The other half of the refreshment committee."

Mr. Ouimet digested this new information slowly.

"William Jones?" he said frowning, his benign smile momentarily erased by what sounded suspiciously like a badly timed joke.

"William *Shakespeare* Jones, sir."

"I don't seem to recall..."

Mr. Landers, who functioned as a vice-principal as well as a math teacher, stepped forward. "Mr. Jones is a transfer student," he said. "He's been with us for only two weeks."

Mr. Ouimet nodded, his smile restored. "I see. Well, Mr. Jones, can you tell us exactly what happened here?"

Without even glancing at Elise, Shakespeare shook his head. "I'm afraid not, sir. I was in the kitchen at the time, but I was busy at the refreshment counter. I'm afraid I didn't see what happened."

"I see," said Mr. Ouimet. He rewarded Shakespeare with a temporary expansion of his smile, then turned back to the two girls. By this time Antoine had removed his jacket and had thrown it over Laura's shoulders.

"So," said Mr. Ouimet, "what we have here is a case of one person's word against another's. Do either of you wish to alter your story at all?"

Laura shook her head vigorously and glowered fiercely at Elise. Elise hesitated a moment, then she too shook her head.

"I see," said Mr. Ouimet. "In that case I have no choice but to punish you both. I will see the two of you in my office immediately after the last class of the day on Monday. Is that perfectly clear?"

Laura nodded, glaring furiously at Elise.

"And you, Miss Chessman?" Mr. Ouimet said.

"Yes, sir. It's clear."

"Fine. I assume there'll be no more mishaps in

the kitchen this evening."

With that, he nodded at Mr. Landers, turned on his heel and the two men left the kitchen.

Miss Everett put an arm around Laura's shoulders and guided her out of the room. Antoine, after pausing a moment to glare in disgust at Elise, followed closely behind.

When they were gone, leaving Elise alone in the kitchen with Shakespeare once more, Shakespeare retrieved a well-used mop from the broom closet and handed it to Elise.

"You know what they say," he said. "You make the mess, you clean it up."

Elise nodded and wordlessly set about mopping the bright red punch off the floor.

At twelve-thirty, the dance was over. Elise stood at the kitchen sink washing the punch bowls. Shakespeare was busy gathering up the used paper plates and cups. By the time each had finished, the gym was silent and empty.

"So," said Shakespeare as Elise dried her hands on a piece of paper towel, "is that it? Can we call it a night?"

Elise nodded. She tossed her paper towel into the garbage can and pulled on her coat. Shakespeare pulled on his jacket and plopped the fedora onto his head.

"Can I walk you home?" he asked as they left the kitchen together.

"No, thanks." It'd been a terrible night. Elise didn't think she could stand having to walk all the way home with a stranger, even a cute one like Shakespeare. He would expect her to make conversation, something she certainly wasn't in the mood for tonight. Tonight she'd lost her very best friend in the whole world. Tonight she'd isolated herself from the one person who'd ever been willing to accept her just the way she was. She didn't feel like doing anything except going straight home and crying herself to sleep in the dark.

"Well," said Shakespeare with a shrug, "I guess I'll talk to you later, then."

"Yeah," Elise replied skeptically, "I guess."

She didn't believe it for a moment.

Chapter 4

When Mrs. Ingram called on Elise in English class at three-twenty on Monday afternoon, Elise didn't hear her. It wasn't until Roger Wendell gave her a poke in the back and she saw Mrs. Ingram peering down at her that Elise was even aware that she hadn't been listening. She'd been too busy worrying about the three-thirty bell.

Elise had tried at least five or six times the previous day to call Laura and apologize. Twice she'd actually picked up the phone to make the call. Once she had even dialled all seven digits of Laura's number and let the phone ring before she broke out in a cold sweat and slammed down the receiver.

In the end she'd convinced herself that if anyone should be apologizing, Laura should be.

If Laura said she was sorry, then, and only then, would Elise also offer an apology. Not before. After all, it was Laura's behaviour that had caused the incident at the dance. If Laura hadn't abandoned Elise the minute Antoine had come on the scene, if she hadn't started treating Elise like a distant second in her life, if she hadn't started strutting around like God's overnight gift to mankind, then none of this would've happened.

But Laura hadn't called, and now Elise would have to go down to Mr. Ouimet's office. And Laura would be there too. Elise would have to face her.

Mrs. Ingram repeated the question slowly, but still Elise couldn't gather her thoughts sufficiently to answer it. Mrs. Ingram said nothing, merely went on to someone else. And though she gave Elise a peculiar look when the bell finally did ring she didn't say anything then, either.

Elise hugged her books to her chest, her shoulders rounded, her head slightly bowed, as she headed slowly to the principal's office. In the corridor a bunch of kids laughed and joked. Shakespeare was at the centre of the group.

Elise sighed. He was so cute. If only he was taller. If only she were shorter. And prettier. And less shy.

It was like wishing she could become a glamorous movie star or a fashion model overnight — it couldn't happen. Suddenly Shakespeare looked up and their eyes met. He grinned widely.

"Hey, legs!" he called, waving at her. All the kids gathered around him turned to look at her. Elise ducked her head even lower. Thank goodness she didn't recognize any of the other faces. Her cheeks on fire, she quickened her pace, eager to get out of sight. How could he have embarrassed her like that?

Maybe he was cute and fun to talk to, but he sure didn't have much sensitivity. How'd he have liked it if she'd called back, "Hi, shrimp!"

The grin would've vanished off his face as quickly as the morning dew under a hot sun. He was just like all the others.

* * *

The principal's outer office was behind a glass wall that formed part of the hallway. When a student was sent to the office, he sat on a wooden bench in the outer office until Mr. Ouimet or one of his vice-principals was able to see him.

Today there were three students cooling their heels on the bench. Two boys from the eighth grade and Laura.

Laura turned her head when Elise opened the door, but she quickly looked away as soon as she saw who it was. Elise sat on the other side of the two boys, as far from Laura as possible. She laid her books on her lap, crossed her hands on top of them and waited.

Minutes ticked by. An office secretary called out a name and one of the boys approached Mr. Landers' office. His face was red and his eyes moist. Probably this was his first trip to the office and he was terrified.

Five more minutes passed and then, at the secretary's call, the second boy arose. He looked anything but nervous as he sauntered towards Mr. Ouimet's office, a cocky grin plastered to his face.

Out of the corner of her eye, Elise peeked at Laura, sitting stiffly on the bench, her eyes star-

ing into space. Elise looked away again, stared at
the clock on the wall and wondered how long
they would have to sit on the hard bench before
finding out how severely Mr. Ouimet intended to
punish them.

Five more minutes passed, then another five.
The nervous boy came out of Mr. Landers' office
with a note in his hand and a look of relief on
his face. Whatever his crime, Elise figured, it
hadn't been serious enough to earn him more
than a detention. If the boy had been punished
more severely he would hardly be leaving with
such a happy expression on his face.

A few minutes later, the cocky boy came out
looking totally deflated. He too had a piece of
paper in his hand, but from the look on his face,
he couldn't have pulled anything less than a
suspension.

Elise drew in a deep breath and squared her
shoulders.

The secretary called out their names and indicated they should both go into Mr. Ouimet's
office together.

Mr. Ouimet was sitting behind his desk, his
hands clasped on the blotter in front of him,
smiling as genially as if he were about to award
them merit badges.

"Close the door, please, Miss Chessman," he
said to Elise. She obeyed, then joined Laura at
the front of Mr. Ouimet's desk. There were two
chairs there, but he didn't invite them to sit
down, so both girls stood.

"Well now, ladies," Mr. Ouimet said, "you've had

two days to ponder Friday night's accident. Do either of you have anything to add to what you've already told me?"

Elise glanced at Laura, who shook her head. Furious, Elise did the same. Mr. Ouimet sighed.

"You know, ladies," he said, leaning back slightly in his chair so that he could look up at them more easily, "I take pride in the fact that I generally know what's going on in my school. I'm not like some principals. I don't just sit up here in my office, cut off from everybody, making policy decisions and handing out detentions. I like to know what's going on. I like to observe. And would you care to know one of the observations I've made over the past few years?"

Elise hadn't the faintest idea what Mr. Ouimet was leading up to, but she decided she'd best play along with him. She looked at him enquiringly.

"I've observed that you two girls are friends. One might even go so far as to say the best of friends."

Again Elise stole a glance at Laura.

"You girls might like to contemplate the fact that friendships are not the easiest thing to cultivate. They are more precious than gold. Wise men and women labour long hours to cultivate and preserve friendships."

Mr. Ouimet stared at each of the silent girls in turn. When he got no response from either, he sighed again and leaned forward.

"I can see I'll have to give you some thinking time. Five hours each in the detention hall — one hour a day for the next five days. You can start now."

Mr. Ouimet handed them slips of paper and dismissed them with a wave of his hand.

Laura left the office ahead of Elise and walked swiftly down the hall towards the detention room, as if she wanted to put as much distance as possible between them. Elise told herself she didn't care.

By the time she'd handed her slip of paper to the teacher on duty, Laura was already in one of the vacant seats, copying a page from a dictionary.

The only other occupant of the room apart from the two girls and the teacher was the nervous looking boy from the office. He also had a dictionary open on the desk in front of him and was working away.

The teacher on duty wrote Elise's name in his roll book along with the number of hours she was to serve and had her sign on the same line. Then he handed her several blank sheets of paper and a dictionary and told her to start at page 245.

Because Laura had started a few minutes before Elise, she was entitled to leave that many minutes sooner. Elise didn't even glance up to see her go. She kept her head bent to her work until her own sixty minutes were up. By the time she'd left the classroom, Laura was nowhere in sight.

For the rest of the week, Elise reported to the detention hall right after the last class of each day, signed in and silently set to work, studiously avoiding Laura's eyes. Every day after her detention she trudged home silently and alone in the early winter darkness.

Elise felt very much alone now. There had always been only Laura. Now there was nobody.

* * *

"Are you sure you don't want to drive into town with us?" Elise's mother asked her on Saturday morning, her head poked around the bedroom door.

"I don't have to be at the clinic until one o'clock," Elise said. "I wouldn't have anything to do downtown until then."

"You could always hang around the university with your father," her mother said.

Elise made a face. That sort of thing had been fun, even exciting, when she was a kid. But now that she was fifteen the idea was boring and babyish.

"I'm not even dressed," Elise pointed out. "Besides, I have a few things I want to do around here this morning before I go."

"Are you sure?"

Her mother looked more concerned than the issue warranted, and Elise couldn't help wondering if it was really something else that was bothering her. Like the fact that Laura hadn't been to the house in the two weeks since they'd gone skating together.

"I'm sure," Elise said. "I can take the bus, no problem."

"What time will you be finished at the clinic?" her mother asked.

"Six o'clock."

Mrs. Chessman winced. "We'll both be through around four. Do you want us to wait for you and drive you home?"

"I thought you were going to dinner at the Normans tonight."

"We are."

"Well, if you have to wait for me and drive me back, you'll be late. I'll take the bus back."

"But, Elise, I don't — "

"I don't mind, Mom. Really I don't. I've taken the bus a million times. It's quite relaxing. I'll just take a book with me and read, that's all."

"You're sure?"

Elise laughed. "I'm sure, Mom. I'll be fine. I'll see you later, okay?"

"I'll call from the Normans — "

"Mom!" Elise protested.

"Just to make sure you got home all right. I'm still your mother, no matter how old you are, and being your mother entitles me to check up to make sure you're safe and sound. You'll understand some day when you're a mother yourself, I promise."

Once her parents had left, Elise dressed and ate a leisurely breakfast of sweet rolls and hot chocolate.

One nice thing about being so skinny, she admitted to herself — probably the only nice thing about it — was the fact that she could eat whatever she wanted, whenever she wanted and not have to worry about it the way other girls did.

By a quarter to twelve she was heading down to Lakeside Drive to wait for the bus into town. The sky was a clear, light blue, the air sharp and icy. As she trudged down the street the dry snow squeaked under her boots.

She'd been standing by the telephone pole that served as the bus stop for less than ten minutes when the big coach lumbered into view. Elise climbed aboard and made her way towards the back where seats were still available. With any luck at all, she'd have a whole double seat to herself so she could stretch out at her leisure for the forty-five minute trip into town.

As soon as the bus pulled away from the curb she opened her novel and began to read. She was still reading when the bus stopped to admit new passengers.

A shadow fell across Elise's page and a voice said, "Excuse me, but is this seat taken?" Elise looked up in annoyance. The bus was half empty. Why was this person imposing on her?

Shakespeare Jones stood there with his familiar grin. Memories of Elise's last encounter with Shakespeare flashed through her head. She sighed. Not only would she have to share her seat, but she'd probably have to put up with "tall" jokes all the way into the city.

She had half a mind to tell him the seat *was* taken. But he was already dropping down into it, lips twitching.

"Well, well, legs," he said as he settled in next

to her, "long time, no see. How have you been keeping?"

"Fine, thank you very much," Elise said stiffly, turning her eyes back to the page of her book and keeping them there, hoping he would get the message that she didn't want to be disturbed, that she intended to read all the way into town, and that if he wanted to sit there, that was fine, but he shouldn't expect any conversation from her.

"I'm fine, too," he said after a few minutes' silence. "Nice of you to ask."

He was teasing her again, she could tell from the tone of his voice. And despite trying not to, she could feel herself blushing.

"So," he said when she remained stubbornly quiet, "how did you make out with our illustrious principal? Did he make you pay for your crime?"

"I got a week in the D-hall," Elise said without looking up.

"And your friend?"

Why didn't he leave her alone?

"She got the same."

"Aha," Shakespeare said thoughtfully. "So you didn't 'fess up, eh?"

That got her attention.

"What do you mean?" she demanded, staring him right in the eye.

Shakespeare shrugged. "I don't know, legs," he said. "I guess I just had you figured for a bigger person, no pun intended. I thought you'd own up and take your lumps like a man, so to speak."

Elise's eyes narrowed. "I don't know what you're talking about," she said at last.

Shakespeare smiled. His pale azure eyes danced over her. "You picked up that punch bowl and overturned it on the other young lady's head. You did it in cold blood, as they say, or in this case, in cold punch, ice and all."

"You said you didn't see what happened!" Elise snapped.

Shakespeare shrugged again. "I lied."

When Elise turned her head away from him and stared out the window, he said, "Don't you want to know why I lied?"

"No," she said, refusing to look at him.

New snow had fallen during the night, dusting everything with its crisp purity. Every twig of every branch of every tree proudly displayed a sparkling cover as soft and downy as angora. Elise wished life could be as beautiful and uncomplicated as it looked at that moment through the window of the moving bus.

"Suit yourself," said Shakespeare, his voice intruding on her thoughts. "But I tell you, if someone had gone to the trouble of covering for me, I'd sure be interested in knowing the reason why."

He wasn't going to let up, Elise could see that. She was going to have to be rude, much as she wished she didn't have to.

"Look," she said roughly, turning from the window and forcing herself to stare at him angrily, "I didn't ask you to do anything. If you felt like lying to Mr. Ouimet, that was your business.

It had nothing to do with me. And quite frankly, Im not only *not* interested in why you did it, I'm not interested in pursuing this conversation any further, either. So kindly leave me alone."

Shakespeare leaned back in his seat and let his fedora slip down over his eyes. Then he crossed his arms over his chest.

Elise watched him for a moment, not trusting him to stay quiet. Finally, when it looked like he really had drifted off to sleep — or was at least trying to — she opened her book again.

"Of course," came Shakespeare's voice before she'd managed to complete even one sentence, "just because you *want* me to shut up doesn't necessarily mean I'm *going* to shut up. It's like the fable about the wind and the sun. Getting all snarly and snappy just has the opposite effect on me to the one intended. The more a person orders me *not* to do something, the more I just naturally want to do it. You know, to see what'll happen."

Elise slammed her book shut angrily.

"Why won't you leave me alone?" she demanded.

Shakespeare straightened up in his seat and pushed the fedora to the back of his head.

"Because," he said, for once not grinning or smirking, "I can't for the life of me think why you want to be left alone in the first place. What are you so angry about? What did I do to make you so mad at me? And what did the girl in the red dress do?"

"It wasn't a red dress. It was a green one."

"Not by the time you got through with it. Look, give me a break, legs. I'm new in this school. Hell, I'm new in this town. Why not be friendly to the new kid on the block?"

Again Elise pictured him in the hallway at school, surrounded by a circle of admirers, everyone laughing at what he was saying.

"I'm sure you can get along perfectly well without me," she said bitterly.

Shakespeare laughed. "I'm sure I can. You know the old song, 'Got along without you before I met you. Gonna get along without you now.'"

Elise could feel her cheeks burning once more. Why did he persist in making fun of her? What was it about her that brought out this twisted sense of humour of his?

Then Shakespeare laid one of his hands over hers. It was warm and dry and soothing. He gave her hand a little squeeze.

"Hey," he said softly, "can't you take a joke? All I meant was, sure, I could manage to make it through life without talking to you ever again. But the point is, do I want to?"

Elise yanked her hand free of his. "Leave me alone," she hissed. "I don't know why you're doing this to me."

"Doing what?"

"Teasing me," she snapped. "Calling me names and making fun of me."

"Calling you names?" he puzzled.

Two creases stretched from one side of his forehead to the other. Then understanding showed in his eyes.

"You mean calling you legs? Hey, I'm sorry. I didn't mean anything by it other than the fact that I think you've got a terrific set of gams. And as for teasing you — I'm sorry, I didn't realize that was what I was doing. What I was trying to do — "

"I don't want to hear it," Elise interrupted, turning her head away.

But still he wouldn't leave her be. He took one of her long, slim hands into his.

"Listen, legs," he said, "I happen to like you. Okay? In my own clumsy way, that's all I'm trying to say. I like you and I wouldn't mind the chance to get to know you better."

"Oh, sure," Elise muttered darkly.

"Honest."

The next thing she knew, one of his hands was coaxing her chin around, imploring her to look at him. Despite herself, Elise let him turn her head — but at the last minute she just couldn't look and she shifted her gaze quickly down to her lap.

"Even after what I did to Laura?" she found herself asking.

Shakespeare chuckled softly.

"I've got to tell you, legs, you're certainly a person who takes the direct approach. And you carried it off with such panache. I don't believe I've ever seen anyone empty a punch bowl over another person's head before, outside of *Three Stooges* reruns."

Elise stole a sideways glance at him. His grin seemed genuine enough.

"And the look on poor Laura's face," he said. He shook his head as he began to laugh even more. "Lordy, Lordy, I don't think she knew what hit her. I wish I'd had a camera."

He was hooting now. A man in the seat across the aisle peered over at them in curiosity.

"I don't know what came over me," Elise said, smiling just a little. "But it sure felt good — at the time."

"And, boy does *that* look good." Shakespeare said as he dried his eyes.

"What?"

"That smile. It's been a long time since I saw that smile. Even that first night, you only smiled a couple of times. You know, you really should do it more often. You're beautiful when you smile. And even cuter when you blush. What's the matter, Elise? Can't take a compliment?"

He'd remembered her name! And he'd used it. He'd called her Elise.

"Where are you going, anyway?" she asked him shyly.

"To an audition," he said. "I'm an actor, remember?"

Elise did remember. An actor. She stiffened and pulled away from him slightly.

"Hey," he protested, capturing one of her hands in his again, "relax. I haven't started acting yet. I'm saving it for the producer. What I said, I meant sincerely."

She blushed and relaxed a little and wondered what was more incredible: that he said he liked her and wanted to get to know her better, or that she was finding herself actually starting to believe it. It couldn't be true. It just couldn't.

For one thing, he was so handsome. She'd never met a boy as attractive as he was. And he was so outgoing, so warm. He'd already attracted a lot of attention at school, yet he'd been there only a few weeks.

Most transfer students had to be around months before anyone noticed. She was willing to bet there were more than a few girls scheming to attract his attention. And here he was, telling her that he was interested in her. It just couldn't be true.

Could it?

Chapter 5

"So," said Shakespeare, settling back into his seat, one of his warm, strong hands holding firmly onto one of her own as if they belonged together, as if they were to be together always, "where are you headed?"

"Red Cross blood donor clinic," Elise answered. "I volunteer down there once a month."

"Giving blood?"

"Giving coffee and doughnuts to the people who give blood. Making them feel appreciated."

Shakespeare smiled. "I bet you do that really well. Going to be there all afternoon?"

"Til six. How about you? How long will your audition take?"

Shakespeare shrugged. "Hard to say. I guess it depends how many people show up. It's kind of a cattle call."

"Cattle call?" It sounded like something that belonged on a farm, not in the heart of the city.

"A cattle call is when a producer issues a general call for actors so that anyone who's interested can show up. It's weird. You walk into an office or onto a stage or whatever and presto, there are twenty, thirty — even a hundred guys

70

who all look roughly the same as you, all going after the same part.

"Sometimes you get a good reading. Other times they shut you up before you can say two words. 'Not the type we're looking for,' they'll say. Or 'too tall.' Or 'too short.' You'll never guess which one I get labelled with.

"Too this, too that, and it's all over before you've shown them what you can do. You're there because you're an actor and you think you can do a good job. You're not there because your nose is long, or because your eyes are big, or whatever. Half the time that's all they notice. I tell you, after a while those rejections can be pretty rough on the ego."

"It sounds terrible!" said Elise. She knew herself what it was like to be judged on looks alone, but she'd never had anything like a job riding on it.

Shakespeare shrugged. A wry smile played across his face. "It's only terrible if you let it get to you, if you let it beat you. Me, well, physically I do have my height going against me. I'm short for a guy and I'm probably not going to grow very much.

"But I also have a good wholesome look — and yet I can look sexy as well when I want to. And I'm a hard worker. I'm creative and determined, and I'm talented. The trick is to get the producer to notice me — to get beyond first impressions."

"That's not easy to do," Elise said drily.

Shakespeare shrugged. "It's not as hard as you

think either," he said. "When I go in for an audition, I go in with a positive attitude. Not, gee, I hope these guys like me. I hope I'm right for them. A lot of guys go in with that attitude, and you know what? When they get turned down, they think it's because they were no good. They feel personally rejected.

"Me, I go in with an attitude that I *am* right for the part and that it's up to me to sell these guys. That's what actors do, right? They're salesmen. They sell an audience emotions, feelings. So my job at an audition is to make sure that the producer gets a good idea of my product, that he doesn't just look at one side of me, the outside and yell 'next.'

"And if I fail, it's not myself as a person who's being rejected, it's my salesmanship that wasn't up to scratch. That's easier to fix than giving myself a whole new body, personality, face, whatever. Right?"

Elise nodded slowly. He had such a positive outlook. Shakespeare exuded self-confidence. But at the same time, there was nothing self-centred or boastful about him. He just seemed honest and matter-of-fact about himself, and that reassured her.

"What's the part?"

"Lead in a kids' play."

"I thought you wanted to be in the movies."

"I do. I'm not there yet, but you never know when one thing may lead to another. And in the meantime, acting is acting. Right?"

"Right."

Shakespeare chatted on so engagingly that Elise was quite startled when the bus finally pulled into the downtown terminus.

They had to go in opposite directions, so they parted company as soon as they got off the bus.

Elise wished Shakespeare the best of luck and noticed with a little pang that he made no mention of seeing her again.

Then, as she stood a moment watching him stride jauntily down the street, she caught a glimpse of her reflection in the bus station window. It took her breath away. She was so big. So tall and skinny. Compared to a man standing nearby, she looked two and a half metres tall.

Maybe that was why, although he claimed to like her, he hadn't actually suggested a date. Maybe he'd been practising his acting after all. Despair surged through her body. What an idiot she was to think he might actually care about her.

Elise sighed to ward off the tears she could feel welling up and marched off in the direction of the blood donor clinic.

She did her best to smile all afternoon as she dispensed the official gratitude of the clinic staff to each donor along with mugs of tea or coffee and fresh-baked doughnuts. But it wasn't easy. Half the time she was thinking moonily of Shakespeare, imagining his grinning face and dreaming of being kissed by him. The other half of the time she was cursing herself for being so foolish, telling herself over and over again to stop daydreaming.

But she couldn't stop. She couldn't get Shakespeare's face out of her mind, no matter how hard she tried.

* * *

By six o'clock the sun had almost sunk below the skyline. It'll be especially cold out there, Elise thought as she stood just inside the foyer of the Red Cross building and buttoned her coat. She wrapped her scarf twice around her neck and pulled on her mittens. Then, bracing herself, she heaved her weight against the door and stepped out into the cold air. The contrast with the heated cosiness of the clinic was so great that she had to gasp for breath. Involuntarily, she ducked her head against the chill as she descended the five concrete steps to the sidewalk.

Elise was concentrating so hard on warm thoughts that she didn't hear footsteps approaching behind her.

A voice said, "Hey, wait up."

She whirled around, her heart pounding in apprehension while her brain told her to cool it, it wasn't very likely that she was going to be assaulted on a brightly-lit street outside the Red Cross clinic.

"Shakespeare!" she exclaimed. He was the last person she expected to see.

He grinned up at her. "I finished early," he said, "so I thought I'd mosey on over and see how you were making out. It's a long bus ride home and I figured, hey, why take it alone when I can have the pleasure of your company. Okay?"

74

Elise beamed at him, conscious, however, that she was looking down at him as she did so.

"Okay."

"I don't know about you," he said, slipping a gloved hand into hers, "but I'm starved. How about we find a nice restaurant and get ourselves a bite to eat before we head home?"

"Gee, I don't — " Elise began, not knowing quite what to say. She'd have just a dollar left after her bus fare was paid. Shakespeare frowned.

"It's only food. I mean, it's not like you have to make a lifelong commitment to me or anything. What's the matter, don't you trust me yet?"

Elise was so startled it took her a few moments to figure out what was wrong. Then she laughed.

"What's so funny?" he demanded.

"You're so beautiful when you're angry," she mocked.

"Thanks a whole lot."

"The thing is, I can't have supper because I don't have any money. Unless you know a place where I can eat for a dollar."

"I see." A smile creased Shakespeare's face and then was replaced by an expression of mock concentration.

"Ah," he said at last, "I know just the place. Come with me."

"You're kidding, right?" Elise asked, allowing herself to be tugged along by his hand.

"My dear legs," he said gravely, "I never kid."

"Sure. And I'll bet you never stretch the truth

a little either."

"Let's walk through the park on our way," he suggested. "Maybe there'll be some people out for an evening stroll."

Elise shivered as a gust of icy wind swirled around her, almost taking her breath away.

"If there are people out," she said through chattering teeth, "I don't think they'll be *strolling*. More likely they'll be *dashing*."

"Even better," said Shakespeare enthusiastically, steering her around a corner and towards a small park dotted with bare trees. The wind swirled through it, whipping snow in little eddies.

Sure enough, people were scurrying along the paths that crisscrossed the square, their heads bent against the wind.

"Perfect," Shakespeare announced.

"Only if you're a polar bear," Elise replied drily.

Suddenly Shakespeare leapt onto a park bench. Elise stared up at him, wondering what on earth he was doing. He winked at her, then his face grew serious, almost brooding, and he began to speak. His voice was soft at first, but it grew louder with each word:

"O, that this too too solid flesh would melt,
Thaw, and resolve itself into a dew!
Or that the Everlasting had not fix'd
His canon 'gainst self-slaughter! O God!
God!
How weary, stale, flat, and unprofitable,
Seem to me all the uses of this world!"

Elise stared at Shakespeare in disbelief. On

one of the coldest nights of the year he was braving sub-zero temperatures and a brutal wind to recite Shakespeare in the middle of a nearly deserted park. Only a madman would do something like that.

Elise looked up at him and shook her head, but by now he was totally wrapped up in his recital of Hamlet's soliloquy. Elise sighed. There was nothing for it — she'd have to indulge his eccentricity. Reluctantly, she wrapped her arms around herself and listened.

Then, to her amazement, Elise found herself becoming less and less aware of the cold and more and more absorbed in Shakespeare's recital. And, she noticed, she wasn't the only one. Several of the scurrying pedestrians had stopped too when they came to the bench.

At first it seemed they were just curious to find out what the oddball on the park bench could possibly be talking about on such a day. But after a few moments, the expressions on their faces changed.

By the time Shakespeare jumped down from the bench, a dozen people had gathered. He was rewarded with a round of appreciative applause.

"Come back in the summer," one older man advised him. "I bet you could make a nice piece of change entertaining the sunbathers."

Shakespeare smiled at the compliment and bowed and doffed his fedora to the crowd. Then he looped his arm once more through Elise's and led her the rest of the way through the park.

"I bet you're good and cold by now," he said,

his own teeth clacking like castanets.

"Why'd you do that?"

Shakespeare shrugged. "I do it as often as I can," he told her. "When I started, it was to get rid of some of my inhibitions. I always wanted to be an actor, but I didn't always find it easy to perform in front of a bunch of strangers.

"Now I like to see if I'm good enough to stop people and grab their interest. Hell, I figure if I can bring people to a halt on a day like today, then there's hope for me."

"True," Elise had to admit. She smiled down at him. "You really are pretty weird, you know."

"Most actors are."

They left the park behind and started down one of the main streets.

"Ah," said Shakespeare, coming to rest in front of a black wrought iron railing, "here we are."

A frozen looking doorman was standing beside a heavy oak door, opening it to admit an elegantly attired man and a woman in a magnificent fur coat.

"You're kidding!" Elise exclaimed.

"Nope."

Elise looked again.

"We can't eat in a place like that," she said.

"Why not?" Shakespeare asked.

"How about because I can't afford it?"

Shakespeare grinned happily. "But I can," he assured her.

"Well, that's nice. But I — "

He silenced her with a wave of his hand.

"It's my treat," he said. "I feel like celebrating."

"You got the part, didn't you?" she asked at last. "I feel so awful! I forgot to ask you how the audition went."

"I got the part," he said calmly. "But even if I hadn't gotten the part, I'd still be taking you here for dinner. Only it would be a consolation prize instead. Every time I have an audition, my mother gives me a pocketful of money so I can either celebrate or ease the pain. Ever since Mom made a name for herself, she's been free with her money and tight with her time."

Elise frowned. She didn't understand, but before she could ask what he meant, they had arrived at the front door of the restaurant. The doorman let them in without a word.

One glimpse of the restaurant's interior convinced Elise she was in the wrong place. She came to an abrupt halt.

"We can't go in here," she whispered to Shakespeare.

"Why not?" he answered in a loud stage whisper. "Do we have a social disease?"

"I'm not dressed."

Shakespeare's eyebrows shot up and he leered at her. Then he adopted an exaggerated look of disappointment.

"But you are dressed," he said sadly.

"I mean I'm not dressed for this place. Look at what everybody's wearing."

Shakespeare shook his head slowly. "My dear legs," he said, "this is a restaurant, not a fashion show."

"They probably have a dress code."

Shakespeare didn't have time to answer. A tuxedo-clad, stiff looking maitre d' approached solemnly. Elise hunched a little, doing her best to make herself as small and inconspicuous as possible, wishing she could vanish entirely. He was going to turf them out, she just knew it. She could tell by the way he was looking at her. Then attention turned to Shakespeare and Elise watched in amazement as the maitre d' beamed affably in recognition.

"Mr. Jones," he said, "how good to see you again."

"Good to see you too, Pierre," Shakespeare said. "Sorry, but I don't have a reservation. Can you squeeze us in?"

The maitre d' smiled again.

"I think we can find a spot for you and the young lady, Mr. Jones," he said, and without further ado, led them to a table in a corner where it was quiet and secluded.

He placed menus in front of each of them and then retired.

"He knows you," she said in awe.

"Yeah," Shakespeare said casually. "That's because my mother has been dragging me to this restaurant regularly for years now. She used to take me on her business trips when we were living out west, and every time we came to Montreal, we always came here."

He had mentioned before something about his mother having made a name for herself.

"Is she famous or something?" Elise asked now.

"To some people I guess she is. For the life of me, I don't know why, though."

"What does she do?"

"She's a writer."

Elise whistled softly in admiration. "That's terrific," she said.

"Not so terrific. She writes romance novels. Do you read romance novels?"

Elise blushed a little. "Sometimes," she confessed.

"Me too. I read my mother's. And believe me, they hardly fall into the category of great literature. But people eat them up. She's made a fortune at it. She gets fan letters from women all over the world. Her stories have even been translated into Chinese. I hear Mom's really hot in Hong Kong."

"It sounds wonderful for her."

"I suppose," said Shakespeare, unfolding his napkin and fiddling with the black-covered matchbook in the ashtray. "But it sure has changed her. She used to be just plain Anita Jones. Then she wrote a book and, whammo, instant success.

"Now she's Anita Jarvis — that's her maiden name. She's divorced from my father and she spends most of her time writing romance novels with a pink-feathered quill pen in lavender ink.

"You think I'm weird? You ought to check out my mother sometime. I don't think they get any weirder without being certified and locked up. Everything in our place is heart-shaped. Pillows, ashtrays, doilies, you name it. Do you have any idea what it's like for a guy to have to take his showers in a pink heart-shaped bathtub? Every day is Valentine's Day at our place."

Elise was giggling. The anguish with which he recounted his tale was so refreshing. Most of the kids she knew would have boasted about it if they had such rich and famous mothers.

"You only think it's funny because you don't have to live with her," he muttered darkly.

"She can't be that bad," Elise said. "She *is* your mother."

He nodded. "Yes, it *can* be that bad, believe me. Don't get me wrong, I love my mom. I just wish she'd get a little better perspective on this romance racket. Football players don't live on a football field. And even the best actors get off stage once in a while."

Elise thought about his performance in the park.

"Is that right?" she asked mischievously.

Shakespeare smiled. "Okay," he said, "but I'm not on now. I mean, if my Mom was here now, we'd be drinking pink champagne and eating lobster purely on account of its colour. And they'd have pink roses on the table, no kidding."

Elise glanced at her menu. "In that case," she said, "you'll be glad to know I'm going to order steak."

Shakespeare grinned happily at her.

* * *

"I hope you're not going to leap up onto one of those benches again," Elise said laughingly as they hurried back through the park after supper. "I enjoyed your act before, but unless I'm mistaken, the temperature has dropped even further."

Shakespeare was smiling at her. "As a matter of fact," he said, "I *was* planning to get up on a bench again." He stopped beside the nearest one and jumped up onto it.

"Great," said Elise wryly. "What do we get now? *MacBeth*?"

"How about this?" said Shakespeare, and without warning he lifted his hat with a flourish and leaned over and kissed Elise on the cheek.

Elise stared up at him. Standing on the bench, he was taller than she was. But that was standing on the bench. Suddenly she felt very foolish. Imagine a guy having to leap up onto something to be able to plant a kiss on your cheek. Boy, would that get the laughs back at school. She pulled away from him.

"That's not funny, Shakespeare," she said sullenly, staring down at the ground.

"It wasn't meant to be funny. It was meant to be a kiss."

When she wouldn't look up at him, Shakespeare jumped down from his perch and stood in front of her.

"What's the matter, legs? Didn't you like it?"

"That's not the point..." Elise began.

She trailed off in frustration. How could she say what she had to say? Why was he making her do it? Surely he could see perfectly well for himself what the matter was.

"What *is* the point?" Shakespeare asked. "I thought we had a pretty good time tonight. I thought you liked me. I know I like you. What's the matter, Elise? Have I been imagining things? Don't you like me?"

"Of course I do. But — "

"But what?" He was standing so close to her now that he had to crane his neck a little to be able to look her in the eye. The top of his head barely reached her chin. Suddenly she felt like a freak again.

"You're making fun of me!" Elise snapped. "You're making fun of me and I don't like it."

"What do you mean, making fun of you?" Shakespeare asked, a startled, hurt look on his face. "What did I do?"

Elise took a step back from him. "Just leave me alone," she said harshly.

"Look, legs — "

"I don't think we should see each other again."

Elise took another step back as he took one forward.

"I mean it, Shakespeare. Stay away from me!"

"What's the matter with me?" he demanded. "What's wrong?"

"It's not you, it's me," Elise blurted out, her voice filled with anguish.

"Come on, Elise, tell me what's wrong. Together we can make it right. Just tell me."

"Stop it!" she screamed.

Elise couldn't believe she was doing it, but she was. She was screaming at the top of her lungs in the middle of the city, not even caring who might hear her, if only he would be quiet and leave her alone.

"Elise — "

"No!" she shouted at him. "I don't want to see you again. I mean it!"

She turned abruptly and ran away through the park, along the streets, dodging pedestrians until her lungs ached from the frigid air she was sucking. Finally she slowed her pace and looked around. He wasn't behind her. He hadn't followed her.

When she reached the bus terminus, he wasn't there either. She boarded her bus and retreated to the back where she sat down in the darkness and began to cry silently.

Chapter 7

When the phone rang shortly after Elise let herself in the front door later that night, her heart skipped a beat. She froze in the hallway in her coat and boots, riveted to the spot, listening to the insistent ringing. It didn't stop. The phone kept ringing and ringing, until finally Elise knew she had to answer it.

She picked up the receiver and said a tentative hello.

"Elise? Elise, is that you? Thank God! I was so worried."

It was her mother. Not Shakespeare at all, but her panicked mother. Elise had forgotten she'd said she was going to call.

"Where were you?" The initial relief that had flooded her voice when she heard Elise answer now gave way to anger. "I thought you said you'd be leaving the Red Cross at six o'clock. It's almost ten now. Couldn't you at least have called me?"

"Sorry, Mom," Elise said quietly. Her voice was shaking.

"Are you all right?" her mother asked. "You sound a little funny."

In her mind's eye, Elise could see the furrows in her mother's forehead. She loved to worry.

"I'm fine, Mom," Elise said. "Just tired, that's all. I stayed longer than I'd planned at the clinic. They were short-handed."

Her mother sighed. Elise wondered where she was in the Norman house. Not in the living room. Elise couldn't hear any other voices in the background, yet the dinner party would surely be in full swing by now. Probably she was upstairs in Mr. and Mrs. Norman's bedroom.

"You work too hard, Elise. It's lovely that you volunteer for things, but I don't think you should overtax yourself. You're still in school, remember? You need your energy for your studies."

"Yes, Mom," Elise said dutifully. "How's the food?"

Now came a click of disgust. "She's doing French, if you can imagine. You'd think she'd know French has been *passe* for a couple of years now.

"Well, get some sleep, dear, and don't wait up. We'll be late."

After she'd hung up, Elise pulled off her boots and coat and headed straight up to her room. Wearily she pulled on her pyjamas and stretched out on her bed.

But she couldn't sleep. She kept waiting for the phone to ring again.

* * *

Elise spent the next morning sitting in her room, telling herself that she'd done the right thing. It just wouldn't have worked out between them. He was so short, she was so tall and still growing. And even if he said it didn't bother him, she knew that eventually it would.

At noon the telephone rang. Her mother was in the bathroom, so Elise went out into the hall and picked up the extension.

She recognized Shakespeare's unmistakeable voice right away and quickly hung up the phone.

A moment later she lifted the receiver off its hook and laid it quietly on the hall table.

* * *

Elise took her time walking to school the next morning, making sure she didn't arrive early enought for Shakespeare to catch her at her locker, if he even knew where it was.

And she made it to homeroom in time to avoid having the Weasel chew her out again, but with too little time for Shakespeare to wait for her there.

As the Weasel was reading out the roll, Carl Martin leaned over and dropped a pink envelope on her desk. Her name was neatly printed on it in lavender ink. She glanced over at Carl, who shrugged, then grinned. Then, as she sat staring at it, wondering who it was from, a shadow fell across her desk.

She scrambled to slip the note inside her geometry text, but she was too late. The Weasel's hand closed around it.

"What," he said loudly, holding the envelope aloft, "is this? Surely there isn't a student in this class who would *dare* to send a note while I am engaged in the task of tracking down truant students by taking roll call."

He stared down at Elise. "Is there, Ms Chessman?"

Elise stared at the surface of her desk.

Thwak!

The Weasel's pointer crashed down onto the surface of her desk, causing Elise to jump out of her seat and utter a small yelp.

"Stand, Ms Chessman," the Weasel ordered.

Reluctantly, Elise stood.

"Please look at me, Ms Chessman."

Elise had to bite her lip to keep it from trembling as she lifted her head and met the Weasel's eyes.

"Now, would you please be so kind as to read this note to the class."

Elise stared at the Weasel. She didn't move. She couldn't. And as she stared, the Weasel inserted a finger under the envelope flap and ripped it open without once taking his eyes off Elise.

"It is forbidden in my class to pass notes," the Weasel said. "This is stated clearly in the student handbook, page 52. I have a copy on my desk which you may consult if you do not believe me. It further states that it is at the discretion of a teacher to confiscate forbidden objects in his or her classroom. Since this note is a forbidden object, I am certainly within my rights to confiscate it."

He pulled a folded sheet of paper from the envelope. Elise had to fight the urge to grab it out of his hands. She'd be expelled if she did that.

The Weasel unfolded the piece of notepaper and held it up, clearing his throat ostentatiously. Elise prayed for an earthquake or a hurricane, anything that would sweep her off the face of the earth instantly and permanently.

"Dear legs," the Weasel began. He paused and looked down at Elise's legs with such exaggerated interest that a couple of kids snickered. Then he took another breath.

"Dear legs," he read, "I need to talk to you. Please meet me in the cafeteria at noon today so we can talk about our relationship. Love, S."

"Well, well," said the Weasel. There was a smirk on his narrow face as he folded the note. "I'm sure we're all dying of curiosity to see who this admirer is, are we not, class?"

Most of the students laughed.

"Should I assign a detail to stake out the cafeteria this noon to see with whom Ms Chessman has a rendezvous? It must certainly be a gentleman of exceptional attributes for Ms Chessman to be so willing to risk a detention."

There was more laughter. Then, mercifully, the bell.

Elise waited as the Weasel slipped the note back into its envelope and dropped it on her desk before he turned and walked away. He said nothing further about punishment.

Elise kept her head down as she fled the room, suddenly seeing the wisdom of the ostrich. She couldn't make herself invisible, she knew that. But at least, if she tried hard enough and refused to look up, she might be able to make herself oblivious to the staring, mocking faces of the kids who had heard what had been meant for her alone. She hated Mr. Nyman with a passion she'd never felt for anyone else. She despised him.

"Elise."

She recognized the voice. It was Laura.

"Elise, wait up. Don't walk so fast."

Elise didn't slow down.

"Elise, that was rotten, what the Weasel did. Look, if you want me to, I'll meet this 'S' for you and give him a message or something, okay?"

"You're not going to trick me!" Elise said sharply to Laura.

"Trick you?"

"Sure. You're just dying to see who'd send me a note like that. Well, forget it. It's none of your business."

"Elise — "

"I said forget it, and I meant it."

"I just thought…Donny and those guys will be hanging around the cafeteria for sure. Probably half the school will."

"Well, I won't be. Now if you'll excuse me, I have a class to get to."

Elise lengthened her stride and soon left Laura behind.

As she walked into her class, Donny Ester-brook said in a loud voice, "Well, if it isn't legs!"

Most of the kids started to laugh. The ones who hadn't yet heard the story of Elise's note were filled in by the ones who had. It was obvious that there'd be an eager crowd in the cafeteria at noon, just as Laura had said, waiting to see who the mysterious "S" was.

Well, let them show up, thought Elise. Let them stand there all afternoon if they wanted to. I certainly won't be there.

Suddenly, in the middle of math class, it occurred to Elise that if Carl Martin had handed her the note, then someone must have asked him to do it. She had to stop Carl telling everyone who had given him the note to deliver.

As soon as math was over, Elise hurried to English. Carl was in the same class. She grabbed him before he could enter the room and yanked him aside, out of the hustle and bustle.

"Who gave you that note?" she demanded. He stared up at her in astonishment.

"Don't *you* know who it's from?"

"That's not what I asked," Elise snapped. "I asked who gave it to you."

"No one."

"What do you mean, no one? It had to come from someone."

"Nobody gave me the note," Carl said. "It was sitting on my desk when I went into class this morning. I guess whoever left it there just left it on the wrong desk, that's all."

"So you have no idea where it came from?"

Elise asked again. "You didn't see who left it there?"

"I already told you I didn't," Carl said in exasperation. "What do you want me to do, sign in blood?"

Elise shook her head. "That won't be necessary," she said. Relief flooded through her.

"Thanks," said Carl sarcastically. "Can I go now?"

* * *

At lunch time, Elise stayed in the library, much to the disappointment of a sizeable number of extra students who had somehow managed to squeeze into the already crowded cafeteria, and at the end of the day, she made straight for her locker, determined to retrieve her things and go home as quickly as possible. But it was not to be.

As she approached the lockers, Elise noticed dozens of people filling the hallway. When she drew closer, they turned to stare at her, parting like the waters of the Red Sea to let her pass.

Standing in front of her locker were two men in olive uniforms. On their jackets were badges indicating they were from a florist shop. Each of the men held two enormous baskets of roses. One had red roses, the other pink. When she stepped forward through the crowd, Donny Esterbrook spotted her.

"That's her," he said to one of the deliverymen. "That's Elise Chessman."

The man with the red roses looked up at her.

"That true?" he asked in a clipped tone. "You

Chessman?"

She nodded.

"Then these are for you," he said. "Look, honey, I don't know whose big idea this was. But I got to tell you, in all my years I never heard of delivering flowers to a high school locker before."

The two men put their baskets down at her feet.

"But what am I supposed to do with them?" Elise protested. The baskets were far too heavy to carry home.

"That ain't my problem," the red rose man said. "We got an order to deliver 'em. They're delivered. The rest is up to you."

He nodded to his co-worker and they departed.

Elise sighed as she stared down at the four baskets. Tucked into one was a small white envelope. Picking it up, she opened it and read the card inside.

It said simply, "Meet me at the theatre at eight o'clock, after rehearsal. S."

When she caught Donny Esterbrook trying to sneak a peek at the note, she hastily slipped it into her pocket. Then she contemplated the roses. What on earth was she going to do with them? She couldn't take them all the way home with her. And if she left them in the hallway all night, they'd simply be wasted. It didn't take much to realize that they must have cost Shakespeare a small fortune. She wished he hadn't done it.

Finally she picked up two of the baskets and

started down the hallway towards the exit.

"Those other two baskets had better be there when I come back," she called over her shoulder to the cluster of bewildered students.

"Wait!" someone called. It was Carl Martin. He ran to catch up with her. "You need some help with those, Elise? No strings attached, honest."

"I'm not going to tell you who sent them, if that's what you're after," Elise warned.

He didn't seem disappointed. "I know. I just thought you could use some help. I didn't mean to get you into trouble with the Weasel, you know."

"Yeah, I guess it wasn't your fault. And yes, as a matter of fact I could use some help. I'm taking these across the street."

Carl's eyes widened. "To the cop shop?"

Elise laughed as she shook her head. "Not across that street. Across Cedar."

Carl nodded enthusiastically. "To the old people's home," he said.

"It might brighten the day for them. I've sure got more flowers than I can use."

"Well, wait up," said Carl, and he retraced his steps down the hall to retrieve the other two baskets.

Together they carried them across the street and into the seniors' residence, where Elise explained to the receptionist that she wanted them distributed to the residents. Before leaving, Carl plucked a couple of red roses and a couple of pink ones from the baskets and handed them to Elise.

"I don't know who this guy is, Elise," he said, "but he must be nuts about you. You should keep at least a few of his roses."

Elise took the flowers. "Thanks Carl. And thanks for your help."

Chapter 7

Eight o'clock came and went and Elise wondered if Shakespeare was disappointed when she didn't show up at the theatre.

By the next morning she was sure, really sure, she'd heard the last of him. She'd snubbed him so many times now, he was bound to give up. In a way, she was sorry it'd worked out the way it had. She *did* like him.

But it was better this way. Elise knew it. There was no way either of them would have been able to put up with the jokes and ridicule they would have had to endure as a couple. People would have laughed. People would have stared. People would have made them feel like freaks. And Elise had already had enough of that treatment to last a lifetime.

She promised herself that if another boy ever expressed any interest in her, she would ignore him totally if he wasn't at least a few centimetres taller than her. Preferably tall enough for her to wear heels.

* * *

At school, things were back to normal for Elise. There was no note on her desk in homeroom, nothing awaiting her at her locker. There was, in fact, nothing out of the ordinary at all.

At lunch time, Elise found a seat in a corner of the cafeteria to eat and read. She sat down and soon lost herself in her book — so much so that she didn't notice the giggles and snickers that began around her.

The giggles became chuckles, and then the chuckles became laughter. Suddenly Elise was aware of a looming presence. When she at last looked up, she almost jumped out of her seat.

Staring down at her from the other side of the table was an enormous gorilla holding a ukelele. At least, that's what she thought at first. When she looked again, she saw it was someone dressed up in a gorilla suit.

Oh, no, thought Elise as she struggled to regain her composure. Now what?

She stared the gorilla right in the eye and said as calmly as she could manage, "Yes? Can I help you?"

"Elise Chessman?" a muffled voice asked.

Elise sighed. "I'm Elise Chessman."

The gorilla grunted and climbed onto a chair. From the chair, he climbed to the tabletop.

"Hey," Elise shouted as she grabbed at her milk, "watch what you're doing!"

An expectant hush fell over students in the cafeteria.

The gorilla took advantage of the silence to begin strumming his ukelele. Then he started dancing on the table while he serenaded Elise with a medley of old-fashioned tunes.

Elise couldn't believe this was happening to her. She gazed into the two human eyes inside the gorilla head, trying to decide if they belonged to Shakespeare.

After a few moments, Elise stood up slowly, ignoring the gorilla soft-shoeing on the tabletop in front of her. Then she repacked what was left of her lunch and started to walk away. The gorilla stopped singing and dancing and the uke-lele fell silent.

"Hey," he rumbled at her, "I haven't finished my routine yet."

The gorilla's protest broke the spell and laughter rocked the cafeteria.

Elise kept walking.

"Hey!" the gorilla shouted at her again. "You can't go. I haven't delivered my message yet."

"Hey, legs!" Donny Esterbrook called from the back of the room. "Hey, don't you want to hear what the monkey has to say?"

The laughter around her redoubled. Elise had wanted to leave the cafeteria calmly, with great dignity, but now she began to run. The laughter behind her swelled to a crescendo.

She raced down the hallway, not caring who saw her or what the consequences might be. Her feet pounded on the tile floor. For a moment she thought her mind was playing tricks on her when she heard a distinct echo to her footfalls. It took a few seconds for her to realize that someone was chasing her.

Elise turned and saw Shakespeare behind her. Panicking, she ducked through a door marked "Ladies — Staff Only." Panting, she leaned against the inside of the door and waited for Shakespeare to go away.

"Elise?" came a tentative voice from the other side of the door. "Hey, come on out, Elise. We have to talk."

"Go away," she shouted between gasps. "I don't want to be humiliated any more. You've done enough already."

"Humiliated?"

He sounded puzzled. But then, she wondered, can you really judge an actor by his voice?

"Go away," she said. "I don't want to talk to you."

"Please, Elise — "

"Go away!"

There was silence on the other side of the door. Then she heard faint, receding footsteps. He was leaving. He was really, really leaving. Elise slid down the door as great sobs began to wrack her body.

Several minutes later, feeling drained and wretched, Elise turned on the cold tap at one of the sinks, determined not to be seen with a tear-stained face. She ducked to the sink and began to splash her face with the cold water.

The door opened behind her.

Quickly she grabbed a paper towel and dabbed at her eyes while she tried to think of an excuse for being in a staff washroom. Apprehensively, she looked in the mirror.

"Shakespeare! You shouldn't be in here!"

Shakespeare shrugged. His hands were jammed into the pockets of his jeans. He didn't look happy. "Neither should you," he said glumly.

Elise stood nervously in front of the sink, twisting the paper towel in her hands.

"I think you'd better leave," she said at last. "Before someone finds you."

He was shaking his head even before she'd finished speaking. "I'm not going until you tell me why you're ducking me. If I have to spend the rest of my life in a ladies' john, I will. Tell me what the problem is, Elise. What have I done that was so wrong?"

Elise stared down at her hands while she continued to twist the paper towel.

"Nothing," she murmured at last. "You haven't done anything wrong."

"You mean you treat innocent people like this?" Shakespeare asked.

"You've ignored me. You've run off from me. You've hung up on me. You've left me waiting in the cafeteria. It's anybody's guess what you did with the roses I sent you — "

"I donated them to the old people's home across the street," Elise interrupted in a whisper.

"Oh." He sounded surprised. "Well, I'm glad somebody got to appreciate them. You obviously didn't. What does a guy have to do to get you to notice him, Elise? Tell me, because I'm running out of ideas. The straightforward approach didn't work and I've used up just about all the gimmicks I can think of — "

"Shakespeare, I don't want to go out with you." There, she'd said it simply and calmly. He'd have to accept that.

"Bet you can't look me straight in the eye and say that."

She forced herself to raise her head and look at him.

"I don't want to go out with you," she said again.

His shoulders sagged. "Why not? What did I do?"

"I've told you. You didn't do anything."

"Then what's wrong with me?"

"There's nothing wrong with you."

"Either I must have done something or there must be something wrong with me, one or the other. You have to have some kind of reason for not wanting to see me. And I'm not leaving here until you tell me.

"You know it's only a matter of time before a teacher walks in here. So you'd better talk to me, Elise, before we both get into trouble."

"Shakes — " She took a step towards the door. He stepped back against it, barring her way.

"There are two ways to get by me, Elise," he said. "Either tell me what's wrong, or force me out of the way. And I've gotta warn you, Elise, I'll put up a fight."

Elise didn't know whether to laugh or cry. She wanted to do both. Then she looked at him and found herself smiling.

"Aha!" Shakespeare said triumphantly. "That's a good sign, right?"

"You're crazy, Shakespeare," Elise said with a sigh.

"But…" Shakespeare added. "I can feel a but coming. I'm crazy, but…"

"It's not you," Elise said at last. "Oh, it's not you at all. It's me. That's the problem."

"But what? What's the problem? There's nothing wrong with you."

"How can you say that?" she demanded, exploding. "Look at me!"

Shakespeare smiled. "I *am* looking. That's why I'm not leaving."

"Look at my height," Elise yelled in exasperation. "I'm way too tall for you."

"I knew it! There *is* something wrong with me. I'm too short!" Shakespeare protested with a silly grin. "That's it, isn't it. That's what you really mean when you say you're too tall for me. You mean *I'm* too short."

"I didn't — "

"Oh, *sure*, you're trying to spare my feelings by saying you're too tall. Okay, if I promise to grow another thirty centimetres, will you go out with me? How about giving me the next month at least while I work on it?"

Elise couldn't keep from laughing. And that was all it took. Within moments they were both doubled over in uncontrollable hysterics.

When they'd recovered, Shakespeare stood up on tiptoe and planted a gentle kiss on Elise's lips.

"You mean it, don't you? You really want to go out with me?" Elise asked.

Shakespeare nodded. "I've been crazy about you from the first moment I saw you. I don't know what happened, exactly, but when I walked into that kitchen and saw you, *something* clicked into place inside me."

"People will laugh at us, you know."

Shakespeare shrugged. "I've always been short." he said. "I've never let my size stop me before, and I don't intend to now. So, how about it? It's up to you. Are you going to let the rest of the world decide what you do? Or are you going to decide for yourself?"

The bell rang outside in the hallway. For a few moments neither of them moved. Then Elise stooped and kissed Shakespeare.

As they left the washroom, she started to laugh.

"What're you laughing at?" Shakespeare asked, looking up at her, puzzled.

"A gorilla!" Suddenly she was laughing so hard again she could barely get the words out. "Why a gorilla?"

Shakespeare grinned. "Well," he answered, "you *are* the gorilla my dreams."

Elise laughed even harder. "Thanks!"

"You're welcome."

Chapter 8

Shakespeare tossed a strawberry into his mouth and closed his eyes in exaggerated rapture.

Then, after he'd swallowed it, he adopted a solemn expression.

"You know," he said to Elise, "I get the distinct impression that you're embarrassed to be seen in public with me."

"That's not true," Elise replied quickly, stiffening as she did so. She had hoped he wouldn't ask about it.

They were in his mother's apartment. It was everything Shakespeare had warned her it would be.

The textured wallpaper in the living room featured pink hearts and red roses. The bases of the lamps standing on the elegant glass end tables were shaped like hearts. The sofa was pink, the overstuffed armchairs white. Ashtrays, candy dishes and doilies were all heart-shaped.

"Ever since we declared a truce in the teachers' loo you've been avoiding me," Shakespeare complained as he reached for another strawberry.

Elise laughed. "How can you say that? I'm

here, aren't I?"

"Only because the rest of the world isn't."

"That's not true. I'm here because I want to be here."

He shook his head as he wagged a scolding finger at her.

"You know what I mean. I get the distinct impression, for example, that you're relieved we're not in any of the same classes. And how come you've been getting me to meet you in the library at lunch time? And for that matter, how come there's always something you have to do right after school that prevents us from walking home together?"

"Can I help it if I'm a busy person?" Elise asked lamely.

Shakespeare studied her a moment. "No," he said at last, "I guess not."

Elise breathed a sigh of relief. But her relief was short-lived.

"So," Shakespeare went on, leaning back casually on the sofa, "we're going to the dance on Friday, right?"

Elise blanched. "Dance? What dance?"

"The Easter dance. At school. The one that's been advertised on humungous posters in every hallway and classroom for the past week and a half."

"Oh," said Elise gloomily, "that dance."

"That's the one."

"I can't. I'm on the refreshment committee."

Thank goodness she'd remembered that. As far as Elise knew, none of the kids at school had figured out who her secret admirer was. She'd managed to keep her personal life just that — personal.

With nothing new happening where Elise was concerned, the kids had begun to lose interest in her. She didn't want to turn that around now and call attention to herself once more.

Shakespeare was grinning. She knew that grin by now. It put her on guard.

"What's the matter?" she asked, smiling uncertainly. What was he going to spring on her, she wondered.

"Nothing."

"Shakespeare! You're up to something, I know it."

He laughed.

"Shakespeare, I'm warning you..." Elise began to stalk towards the sofa like a panther. "Tell me, or suffer the consequences."

She jumped on Shakespeare and began to tickle him.

"Uncle, uncle!" he cried after a few moments.

Elise sat on his chest and held his arms down over his head.

"Speak up, then," she said threateningly. "Tell me what's up — or I start tickling again. I'm warning you, these fingers are registered with the police. They're classified as dangerous weapons."

"Okay, okay. Just don't tickle."

"Then talk."

"You're not on the refreshment committee."

Elise laughed. "Nice try, Jones," she said, "but I

am on the refreshment committee. I *am* the refreshment committee."

He shook his head silently. Beneath the smile she saw a seriousness that scared her. She released his hands and got up.

"I have a responsibility to the refreshment committee. I can't just turn my back on that. I've got a job to do and people depend on me to get it done."

"Nice try, legs," Shakespeare replied.

The hint of sarcasm in his voice prevented her from protesting further. She watched him in silence as he sat up and looked at her.

"Don't hand me that stuff about your responsibility to serve sandwiches and punch, because I don't buy it. People will just have to depend on some other happy homemaker for a while."

"But — "

"I'm not finished, Elise. This is serious. It just so happens that I handed your resignation in to Mrs. Ingram last week."

"What? You had no right to do that!" Elise shouted at him.

"Well sue me then, because I did it. I told Mrs. Ingram that for once you were going to a dance to dance, not to wait on everyone else. And you know what she said? She said she thought that was a terrific idea. She said she thought you were a nice girl and that it's about time you started to have a little fun. I said I thought so too. So now there's a new refreshment committee and you're not on it. Which means you're free to go to the dance with me."

"You shouldn't have done that," Elise said again in a quieter voice. "That was none of your business."

"Wrong! I happen to care about you, Elise."

"If you cared about me, you wouldn't go sneaking around behind my back, handing in resignations without asking me."

Shakespeare sighed. "That's not the point, Elise," he said softly but firmly, "and you know it."

"I don't know what you're talking about."

"I'm talking about your fear of being seen in public with me. You know I'm right. You think something terrible is going to happen if we're seen together. I don't know what — except that maybe you think people will get a chuckle out of the difference in our heights — "

"A chuckle?!" Elise grabbed her coat and turned on him. "A chuckle? Is that all you think they'll get out of it? I've been through this before, you know. I know what it feels like to be the circus freak, to be the giant everyone wants to gawk at. I've done it before and I don't want to do it again, thank you very much!"

He laid a hand on her arm gently.

"I've been through it before too, you know. It's no big deal."

"It is to me!"

"But, Elise, if you make it into a big deal, that's *your* problem, not everyone else's. You can't go around blaming other people. If you insist on being miserable, that's up to you. But don't pretend other people are forcing the misery on you, okay? It'll only make things more difficult for you. Believe me, I know."

Elise glowered at Shakespeare. Then, her hand on the front door, she said, "Nice speech, Shakespeare. But I'm leaving."

She slammed the door behind her, her hand trembling. She hurried down the hallway to the fire exit, unwilling to wait for the elevator.

Shakespeare had no right to do what he'd done, she thought bitterly. And he had no right to lecture her about what she should or shouldn't feel.

She began to pound down the stairs. It was a long way down — Shakespeare's mother lived in the penthouse.

What did Shakespeare know about being a giant anyway? Nothing, that's what. For one thing, he was anything but tall. Elise would have given her right arm to be as small as he was.

Of course, for a guy, Shakespeare *was* a bit off the optimum height. Okay, so for a guy he was a shrimp — and that must have been hard on him. But not so you'd notice. If there was one thing that Shakespeare seemed oblivious to, it was height — both hers and his.

But then, why shouldn't he be? After all, apart from being small, he was handsome and talented. The guy was an actor, for Pete's sake. So what did it matter that he was short? As he'd already pointed out to Elise, there were plenty of short actors around and they got plenty of good roles. So being short wasn't necessarily a handicap, as long as you had something else going for you.

But being a girl and being tall *and* being just ordinary in every other way, now there was a handicap. The only thing that distinguished Elise from about a million other girls was the fact that she was so much taller than them. Not prettier or smarter or more talented. Just taller. Freakier. Gargantuan. Extra large.

So what? She heard a voice that sounded suspiciously like her own ask in the back of her mind. So what?

Elise stopped dead in her tracks and sat down on the step.

"Darn it all," she said out loud as she stood again only moments later and slapped the railing with the palm of her hand. "Darn it all. He was right. Shakespeare was right."

The words echoed in the empty stairwell as Elise slowly descended to the next landing.

There was no one in the hallway when she got off the elevator, but the moment she knocked on Shakespeare's door it flew open and he was standing there, smiling at her.

"I knew you'd come back," he said, wrapping his arms around her.

Chapter 9

"But who is this boy?" her mother asked when Elise came downstairs in a new dress — a pale blue gown with a full skirt.

"I told you, Mom, his name is Shakespeare Jones." Elise went directly to the mirror over the small chest of drawers in the hallway and began to fuss with her hair. It didn't look right somehow. Nothing looked right.

"Don't tug at your dress like that," her mother said. "You'll ruin it. And what kind of name is that anyway, Shakespeare?"

"His mother's a writer," Elise said. "Maybe you've heard of her. Anita Jarvis."

She knew for a fact that there was a half-read Anita Jarvis novel on her mother's bedside table. Her mother's eyes widened in surprise.

"*The* Anita Jarvis?" she asked, her voice full of awe. Elise nodded. "Well, I'll be. Still, I don't think you should be going out with boys your father and I have never met."

"You'll meet him in a few minutes," Elise said, "when he comes to pick me up."

Her mother didn't look happy. She stood behind Elise, hands on her hips, frowning.

"Mom, it's a school dance. We'll be chaperoned to death."

Her mother sighed. "I know," she said. "It's not that..."

"What, then?"

"I don't know." Suddenly her mother turned away and lifted a hand to her eyes.

"Mom?" Elise turned from the mirror and laid a hand on her mother's shoulder. "You're not crying, are you?"

"Don't be silly," her mother said. But she didn't turn to look Elise in the eye right away. And when she finally did, it was with a trembling smile on her lips and reddened eyes.

"It's just that, well, this *is* your first real date, you know."

"Yes, I do know," Elise said with a dry laugh. "I don't think I've ever been so nervous in my whole life. But don't worry, I'm not planning to marry Shakespeare — at least not yet. And you'll like him, Mom, I know you will."

Just then the doorbell rang. Elise froze. The time had finally come. Any moment now she'd walk out the front door on her way to a dance with a date a great deal shorter than she was. It wasn't going to be easy.

"Get your coat, dear," her mother said softly, giving Elise a little push. "I'll answer the door."

Shakespeare introduced himself to Mrs. Chessman while Elise slipped on her coat. When she stepped into the vestibule, her mother was smiling approvingly at Shakespeare.

Her expression didn't waver when Elise took

her place by his side.

"Well, be home at a reasonable hour," she said, going up on tiptoe to kiss her daughter on the cheek. "And have a good time."

"We intend to, Mrs. Chessman," said Shakespeare exuberantly. Elise said nothing.

Shakespeare took her hand and led Elise to a waiting taxi.

"Isn't this a little extravagant?" Elise asked apprehensively as he held the door open for her.

"Well, I don't drive, so my mother thought it would be romantic if I hired a taxi." He slid into the back seat beside her and gave the driver directions to the school.

They drove in silence, Elise clinging to Shakespeare's hand as she told herself over and over again that she could do it, it wasn't going to be the end of the world, no matter who said what.

"You okay?" Shakespeare asked eventually, frowning as he tried to peer into Elise's eyes in the gloom.

Elise managed a weak little smile as she nodded in response. Someone was bound to say something. Out loud. Probably even to her face. Someone like Donny Esterbrook or Bobby Elliott. They'd both be there.

One wisecrack, and their evening together would be ruined. Elise knew right there in the taxi that she just wouldn't be able to handle any smart comments. She'd feel as though everyone were staring at her, as indeed they probably would be. Her humiliation would be complete.

"You sure you aren't nervous or anything?"

Shakespeare asked. Once more she shook her head. "Good," he went on, "because I'm terrified. But as long as you remain cool, I've got nothing to worry about."

That did it. "Terrified?" she asked. "You? What are *you* terrified of? You think people are going to laugh at us, don't you? You think that because I'm so tall — "

"Legs, honey, height is the least of my problems, I assure you. Look, I should've told you this before — "

"What? What is it?" she demanded anxiously.

"Have you ever seen me dance? No, of course you haven't. Well, look, when it's time for us to get out there and boogie, I want you to promise me one thing. Just be kind to me, legs. Whatever anyone else says or does, be kind and remember I'm trying as hard as I can, okay?"

He was so solemn, his voice so tremulous, that she had to laugh. Shakespeare sniffed in indignation.

"And all this time I thought you had a sensitive soul," he complained. "Oh, how could I have misjudged you so badly?" He threw an arm up over his face, and suddenly Elise wasn't sure whether he was kidding — or just pretending that he was kidding to hide the fact that he really was hurt.

"Shakespeare, I'm sorry," she said quickly, pulling his arm away from his eyes. Then, when she saw the impish glint, she gave him a shove.

"You're making fun of me," she complained.

"I'm making fun, period," he said. "But

seriously, I'm not as well-acquainted with dance floors as I might be. So don't expect Fred Astaire, okay?"

When they arrived a few minutes later, they hurried into the school out of the cold. Shakespeare helped Elise off with her coat like a real gentleman and whistled softly when he got a good look at the dress beneath.

"You look sensational," he told her.

"You don't look too shabby yourself," she answered when he took off his coat to reveal an ultra fashionable suit and tie.

"That's Mom again," he said with a wry smile. "She thinks fashion isn't just something for women. She says men have to pay attention to these things too. Especially men who want to be actors."

"You're such a good son," Elise teased him. "Most guys I know don't listen to a word their mothers say."

"Most guys you know don't have my mother for a mother," he retorted. "At least, I hope they don't. Besides, Mom knows what's she's talking about. Since she became famous, she's met quite a few actors. She's got connections, you know. So I figure she can't be all wrong. Not all right, either, for that matter, but certainly not all wrong. Anyway, you like the suit, huh?"

Elise grinned. "I love it. The only problem is, I think you look a whole lot better than me. You're cuter. You're better dressed..."

Shakespeare laughed. "You sure know how to flatter a guy, legs. But I know what I like and, believe me, I like what I see. So...shall we?"

He held out his arm. Elise took a deep breath, then allowed him to lead her through the door and into the gym.

There was a large crowd already gathered inside, but although the music was blasting out, no one was dancing. It was too early. Elise knew from years of watching from the kitchen that it took a while for things to get started.

For the first hour or so, kids would line the four walls of the gym and gather around the food, talking and watching. Mostly watching, checking out who was there and who wasn't, who was with whom, and what everyone was wearing.

Every detail was noted and discussed. There was no doubt in Elise's mind as she entered the gym on Shakespeare's arm that her presence was being duly commented upon. She only wished she had no idea what people might be saying. But, of course, she did know.

"What say we mosey on over to the punch bowl?" Shakespeare suggested. "For a drink, I mean — not a bath."

"Very funny," said Elise out of the corner of her mouth. "It's not as if I make a habit of doing that sort of thing, you know."

"It's not as if you explained it to me either," said Shakespeare. "Not that it's any of my business, of course."

"Of course." Elise gave him a cynical glance.

"Okay, so I'm dying of curiosity. But that doen't mean I want an instant replay, so control those itchy fingers when we get there, okay?"

Elise started to laugh. Then she glanced over at the refreshment table and stopped in midstride. Standing in front of the punch bowl, her hand looped through Antoine's arm, was Laura.

"I can't go over there," Elise said.

Shakespeare frowned up at her. "Why not?"

"I just can't." She retreated a few paces, closely followed by Shakespeare.

"What's the matter, Elise?" he asked. "We made it this far. Let's just have a good time, okay?"

"I don't want to go near that punch bowl. Not as long as she — "

Elise broke off suddenly, not wanting to explain.

Shakespeare turned and looked over at the refreshment table. "I get it," he said. "Your enemy is there and you don't want to do battle, right?"

Elise was staring at the table. Laura suddenly looked away from Antoine and over to Elise.

Elise smiled at her former friend, ready to close the gap between them. They could have so much fun at the dance together. Then Antoine moved and Laura quickly turned back to him, her face set and impassive.

The smile faded from Elise's face. Without a word, she turned and fled from the room.

* * *

By the time Shakespeare found Elise, she had her coat on and was hurrying towards the nearest exit.

"This is getting to be quite a habit with you,"

he said as he raced up to her and pulled her to a halt.

"Let me go!"

Elise tried to jerk her arm free from his grip, but this time he held firm.

"You're hurting me."

"Then stop struggling," he said calmly.

"I want to leave."

"I don't think that's a very good idea."

"I don't care what you think."

"That's not true," said Shakespeare. "You do care what I think. That's why we're here together, remember. So why don't you stop being so stubborn and tell me what's the matter?"

Elise considered telling him nothing was the matter, but one look at him and she knew he wouldn't believe her. She clamped her mouth shut and said nothing.

"Okay," said Shakespeare. "Then let me tell you what's wrong. Or at least, make a stab at figuring it out."

She glared defiantly at him, telling herself she didn't care what he said or did, there was no way she was going back into that gym.

"Let's see now. You don't want to go back in there because you're afraid of meeting your friend. Or should I say your ex-friend?

"I'll bet dollars to doughnuts that you and what's-her-name were once the best of buddies. After all, one doesn't go around dousing just any old bod in ice cold punch in public. That's the kind of treatment reserved for people who've really hurt you.

"Now here you are, in danger of coming face to face with your victim, and you just can't handle it."

Elise glowered at him. "Do you have a speech for every occasion?" she demanded.

"Do you have an excuse for every occasion?" he shot back. Then he softened.

"Look, Elise, I'm not asking you to do anything more than come back into the gym with me and enjoy the dance. Don't let some dumb fight with an ex-friend spoil our fun."

"It wasn't a dumb fight," Elise muttered stubbornly. "Laura deserved what she got, every last drop."

She bit her lip. "We *were* best friends. You were right about that. But she dumped me."

"Before or after that little tiff in the kitchen?"

"Before. She got a boyfriend, you see, and — "

Shakespeare smiled up at Elise. "And now you've got one too." He reached up and touched her lips with his.

"This was different though," Elise said, blushing. "Laura and I used to do everything together, right from the time we met in second grade. We were inseparable. We took all our classes together, we went to camp together, we joined the same clubs and committees."

"Until some guy muscled his way into the picture, huh?"

"Not quite," Elise admitted. "I guess the trouble really started last summer. I went to camp, as usual, but instead of sending Laura too, her parents decided she'd benefit from a summer in

120

Europe.

"Her father has a brother in England, so he sent her over there and she and a couple of her cousins toured around Britain and the continent. When she came back — well, Laura used to have a weight problem. She was a real butterball. You should have seen us together. We looked like a baseball and a bat."

"The girl in the raspberry punch didn't look so chunky to me," Shakespeare said.

"Right. She must have lost about fifteen kilograms over the summer. The next thing I knew, boys were falling all over her and pretty soon she was so heavily involved with this creep Antoine that I didn't see her anymore.

"We always used to do the refreshment committee together. Always. Only that last time, she told me the day of the dance she wasn't able to do it. Instead, she was going to the dance with Antoine. I guess I was jealous."

"I guess," said Shakespeare. "Question is, who were you jealous of, and why?"

Elise stared at him. "Jealous of Laura, of course. Because she had a date and I didn't."

"You sure?"

"Of course I'm sure."

"It sounds more complicated than that to me. I think you're jealous of Laura all right — but not just because she had a boyfriend."

"So who are you all of a sudden?" Elise demanded. "Sigmund Freud?"

"Hey, calm down. I'm just trying to help."

"How? By psychoanalysing me? No thanks!"

"I think you hung around together in the first place because you were outcasts together." Shakespeare continued doggedly. "The two freaks. The fat one and the tall one.

"Then, presto, Laura betrayed you by shedding her handicap. But there isn't anything you can do to shed what you insist on seeing as your handicap — your height.

"I think you resent the fact that now she fits your idea of normal and you don't."

He reached out and took both her hands in his. "Tell me if I'm wrong," he said. "But don't tell me I'm wrong if you know I'm right. Before you can deal with a problem, you have to identify it. And to do that, you have to be honest with yourself."

Elise was concentrating on the speckled tile at her feet.

"I think maybe you also resent Antoine for taking your place in Laura's life. But suppose you'd met me before Laura met Antoine. Wouldn't you have hoped that Laura would like me? I'm sure Laura hoped the same thing about you."

"She did not!" Elise cried. "She dumped me! She just all of a sudden didn't care about me anymore."

"Maybe."

"Why don't you believe me? Why are you bending over backwards to make Laura look so wonderful? The way you tell it, you'd think she was a saint!"

Shakespeare sighed. "Friends are important,"

he said at last. "Everybody needs friends, and everybody should have a best friend. You and Laura have been friends for — what — nearly ten years. Are you really going to let someone come between you now? Do you really want to throw ten years of friendship away?"

Tears filled Elise's eyes. "I never wanted that," she said. "I didn't want to stop being Laura's friend. It was Laura who stopped wanting to be my friend. She didn't have time for me anymore."

"Maybe she's changed her mind."

"It sure doesn't seem like it," Elise sighed, thinking of the scene in the gym. "And if she has, all she has to do is tell me."

"Maybe she's afraid to."

"Why should she — " Elise began, then stopped. "You're saying I should take the first step, aren't you? But what if she tells me to get lost? Maybe she just isn't interested."

"Maybe." Shakespeare agreed. "But, still, it's worth thinking about. Meanwhile, we could be dancing. I hear it does wonders for taking your mind off things."

Elise groaned. "You really want me to go back in there, don't you?"

"I do. For my sake. What you do once you get in there, besides dancing with me, is up to you."

Elise slipped her hand into his. "I don't suppose you'd consider being my best friend as well as my boyfriend, would you?" she asked softly.

"Only if the job isn't already taken." Shakespeare squeezed her hand and led her back towards the gym.

Chapter 10

Elise held tightly to Shakespeare's hand as she approached the refreshment table. She'd spotted Donny Esterbrook the moment she stepped back into the gym. He was standing to one side of the door as they entered. When he saw her, he looked first startled, then amused.

He's not going to leave me alone, Elise thought. He's going to say something to embarrass me.

It took a great effort to resist the urge to flee, or to hunch her shoulders in an effort to look small, but she managed it. Instead she forced herself to stand straight and tall and to look as proud of Shakespeare as she was. She ignored Donny Esterbrook as she headed straight for the refreshment table.

"Punch?" Shakespeare asked her when at long last they'd completed the trek across the floor.

"Please," said Elise.

She glanced around and once again her eyes met Laura's.

Laura was openly staring at her. For a second, Elise considered smiling again in a bid to take that first step. But she didn't. It was too big a risk. And besides, she still felt that it was Laura who'd been in the wrong. If there were any fences to mend, the first move should come from her.

Laura continued to gaze at Elise a little longer, then looked away. A moment later she and Antoine moved away from the refreshment table. Elise felt an emptiness inside and wished she'd said something, anything.

"Here you go," Shakespeare was saying, and she turned just in time to accept a cup of punch from him. They moved to one end of the table and stood talking to each other quietly as the gym filled up.

Maybe this wasn't going to be a nightmare after all, Elise thought as the evening warm up and the dancing began. People had been looking at her and Shakespeare, and there were more than a few curious glances, to be sure. But no one had actually said anything.

She was just starting to relax when Shakespeare asked her to dance. The disc jockey was playing a soft slow song and out on the floor couples were swaying quietly to the music.

"Correct me if I'm wrong," Shakespeare said as he took the punch cup from her hand and set it on the nearest table, "but this *is* a dance. And at dances, people dance. And since we *are* people..."

He had Elise by both hands and was leading her gently out onto the floor — and to her surprise, Elise was allowing herself to be led.

Shakespeare slipped one arm behind her back. He caught one of her hands in his and drew her tightly to him. Then he began to sway in time with the music, his head resting on her shoulder.

Elise was rigid with embarrassment. All around her, girls rested their heads on their boyfriends' shoulders, and here they were, doing the same thing in reverse.

"Come on, legs," Shakespeare said gently, "loosen up a little. You're supposed to be enjoying this."

But she wasn't enjoying it at all. Elise felt as if everyone was staring at them. Wherever she looked, she saw mocking, laughing eyes. Her cheeks were afire. She knew her face was the colour of the raspberry punch she had poured over Laura. She shifted her gaze downward — to rest on the top of Shakespeare's head.

This is a mistake, Elise thought miserably. I should never have come. I should never have let him talk me into this. Her legs longed to run, to carry her away from the prying eyes. But she forced herself not to give in. She knew in her heart that she just couldn't turn tail and flee and leave Shakespeare alone to face the mockery. It wouldn't be right. She couldn't hurt him like that.

She took a deep breath and smiled down at Shakespeare, and he smiled back. Then, as he nestled down once more against her shoulder, she stared slowly around the room, defiantly meeting every pair of curious eyes, her ferocity forcing them to look away.

By the end of the song she had triumphed — over herself, and over the crowd of curious onlookers. True, she was still tall and people would still talk, but at least they wouldn't say anything to her face.

When Shakespeare suggested they stay on the dance floor for the next dance, she agreed happily. But suddenly she saw Donny Esterbrook making a beeline for them with an ugly grin on his face.

"On second thought, maybe we should sit this one out," she said hurriedly to Shakespeare, trying to edge towards the wall.

"No way," he objected. "I'm just getting warmed up. Look, I know..."

Just then Donny Esterbrook's hand fell on Shakespeare's shoulder. Shakespeare had to look up to see who it was. Donny was only a couple of centimetres shorter than Elise.

"This is a whole lot of lady, sonny," Donny said to Shakespeare. "She needs a man to dance with, not a shrimp."

"Get lost, Donny," Elise growled.

"Put a lid on it, stretch," Donny snarled. "I was talking to the shrimp here."

Shakespeare didn't move. "Get lost," he said simply.

"Get lost?" Donny echoed. He glanced around at his friends and started to laugh.

"Hey, did you hear that? The shrimp told me to get lost!"

He turned back to Shakespeare. "Look, shrimp, if stretch here wants to come out dancing with us, don't make her problems any more obvious than they already are by asking her to dance with you. Okay? It's not nice."

Shakespeare shrugged and looked at Elise. "You want to dance with this jerk?" he asked.

Elise shook her head.

"Right. There's your answer," Shakespeare said to Donny. "So why don't you go back to holding up the wall and leave us alone?"

Donny guffawed. "Get this guy," he called to his friends. "He's a regular wiseguy."

Then he turned to Shakespeare and growled, "I hate wiseguys."

"That figures," Shakespeare said affably. "People of low intelligence often resent their superiors. It's a well-documented phenomenon."

Donny clenched his fists. This wasn't going the way he wanted it to all. The guy was making him look stupid.

Elise glanced around the room.

Chaperones are like taxis, she thought with an inward groan. There's never one around when you need one. She reached out and touched the sleeve of Shakespeare's jacket.

"Let's go," she said quietly. "I think I've had enough dancing for one night."

"I haven't," Shakespeare said. "I plan to dance all night."

"Shakespeare, please..."

He wheeled around to face her. "You can go if you want, Elise," he said calmly, "but I'm not moving. I've as much right to be here as anyone else, including this buffoon."

"Who're you calling a buffoon?" Donny demanded.

By now a small crowd had gathered around them, and still there was no teacher in sight.

Donny waved a fist under Shakespeare's nose. "Step outside, shrimp, and I'll show you who's the buffoon around here."

Elise tugged at Shakespeare's arm. "You can't fight him," she said. "He's twice as big and twice as heavy as you."

"Look on the bright side," Shakespeare replied with a grin. "He's only got half the brains."

"Maybe. But I don't think that counts a whole lot in a fight. Let's just walk away from this, okay?"

"Come on, shrimp," Donny said. "Come on, let's see what all those brains of yours look like spattered on the sidewalk."

"Yeah, yeah," Shakespeare said.

He turned to Elise. "I have to," he told her. "I've no choice."

"If you fight him, you won't have a chance."

"Not necessarily."

"He'll flatten you."

Donny stepped forward. "You two going to yak all night?" he snarled. "Or are you" — looking at Shakespeare — "going to come outside and show me what you can do?"

"Don't do it, Shakespeare," Elise said again.

Without warning, Shakespeare wheeled around and made a feint at Donny. Donny sprang back and then leaped forward and took a swing at Shakespeare. Shakespeare ducked and Donny twirled like a top. As he whirled by, Shakespeare stuck out his foot and Donny fell to the ground with a hard thud.

Shakespeare turned to Elise. "Not bad, eh?" he said, dusting off his hands in an exaggerated fashion, a big grin on his face. "My first fight, too."

But before she could say a word, Donny struggled to his feet and launched himself full force at Shakespeare's back. The impact sent Shakespeare crashing to the floor. When his body came to rest, Shakespeare didn't move. Elise let out a scream and ran to his side.

A crowd immediately formed around them. And then, suddenly there were teachers, lots of them. They appeared out of nowhere, like ants at a picnic.

Mrs. Ingram was the first to bend over Shakespeare. Then Mr. Ouimet was down on his knees beside the limp body. Elise knelt too, tears tracing a path down her cheeks.

Slowly Shakespeare sat up. Then his eyes opened and a grin split his face. He looked at Elise and said, "On second thought, maybe I'm not quite ready for life as a professional scrapper." He rubbed his head with one hand.

"Are you all right, son?" Mr. Ouimet enquired. Shakespeare nodded.

"There's a bump on the back of my head," he said, wincing as he touched two fingers gingerly to the back of his skull.

"Better let me take a look at that," Mrs. Ingram said.

She knelt beside Shakespeare awkwardly — by now it was obvious she was expecting a baby —

and parted his thick hair with her fingers.

"The skin isn't broken," she announced, "but there's quite a bump. Better come in the kitchen with me and let me put some ice on it."

Mr. Ouimet helped Shakespeare to his feet. Before he handed him over to Mrs. Ingram, he told both boys they'd be expected to appear in the principal's office on Monday afternoon. Shakespeare nodded. Donny scowled.

While Shakespeare sat on one of the tables in the kitchen and Mrs. Ingram looked for a clean towel, Elise filled a small bowl with ice. Mrs. Ingram folded them in the towel and applied the ice pack to the back of Shakespeare's head. He winced again, but said nothing.

"You know, Shakespeare," she said as she held the ice against his head, "when you first came to this school I looked at your transcript and said to myself, well, this is going to be a quietly intelligent young man. Your grades were so good, especially in English."

She shook her head as she removed the ice pack for a moment and inspected the bump.

"I guess a transcript doesn't say it all, does it?"

"I beg your pardon, Mrs. Ingram," Shakespeare said politely, "but I'm not sure I understand what you're getting at."

Mrs. Ingram smiled. "Never in all my years of teaching have I seen any one student make such a stir in such a short period of time. Almost as soon as you set foot in this school, I doubt there was a single student who didn't know you — or at least know of you. And the gossip around the teachers' lounge is that you've managed to shake up every single class you've been in with your humour and your impersonations. After the first few days I was convinced you were going to be a giant headache."

"Well, you weren't far wrong, Mrs. Ingram," said Shakespeare. "I don't know whether you still think I'm going to be a giant headache, but I can tell you right now, I do certainly *have* a giant headache."

Mrs. Ingram laughed. "You should've told Mr. Ouimet that you won't be in on Monday. He'll be on the rampage when you don't show up in his office as ordered."

"I'll make sure he knows," Shakespeare promised.

"Knows what?" Elise asked. "Where are you going to be on Monday?"

Shakespeare blushed. "I have to go out of town, Elise."

"Out of town," Mrs. Ingram sniffed. "Please, Shakespeare, don't add modesty to your list of questionable virtues. In spite of the almost daily disruption of my class that you've managed to engineer, I'm going to miss you. I wish you'd been able to stick around longer."

Now Elise was really alarmed. "*Where* are you going, Shakespeare?" she asked again.

"It's nothing — " Shakespeare began.

"Only if you're not impressed at being in the presence of a future Hollywood star," Mrs. Ingram interrupted with a grin.

Then she looked at Elise and her smile faded.

"I" — she glanced at Shakespeare — "I hope this wasn't a secret."

"You're going to Hollywood?" Elise demanded.

"I was going to tell you, legs, really I was," Shakespeare said as he reached for her hand. Elise sprang back out of his way.

"Oh dear," said Mrs. Ingram. "I'm so sorry. I thought…"

"You're leaving and you didn't tell me?" Elise cried. "How could you do this to me? How could you keep it a secret from me?"

Shakespeare jumped down from the table and took a step towards her. Elise took a step back.

"I *was* going to tell you," he said.

"How? In a postcard?"

"I was going to tell you later."

"You're leaving the day after tomorrow." She stared at him. Then a flash of recognition gleamed in her eyes. "That's what all that 'best friend' stuff was about, wasn't it? 'Boys will come and go in your life, but a good girlfriend can be with you forever.' That's what that was all in aid of. What were you trying to do, Shakespeare, sneak away with a clear conscience so you could tell yourself the friendly giant was taken care of, that you didn't have anything to worry about or feel guilty about? Is that it?"

"Elise, please — "

"No." She stiffened. "I'm going home. This time I *am* going. And I don't want you to stop me or come after me or call me. I don't want to see you again. Ever. Understand?"

Elise turned away, but before she could take a

step, he grabbed her by the elbow and turned her toward him. She opened her mouth to protest, and instantly he covered it with his. He kissed her long and hard, wrapping his arms around her in front of Mrs. Ingram, the refreshment committee and anyone in the gym who looked. Her anger dissipated and she felt suddenly and delightfully empty-headed.

"I love you, legs," Shakespeare said when they parted. From the gym came a burst of applause and a spate of whistles. Elise looked around and saw that at least half the students had crowded around the entrance to the kitchen. For once she didn't mind being the centre of attention.

Chapter 11

They stood silently at the end of the Chessmans' driveway. Shakespeare had slipped his arm around Elise's waist while they watched for Shakespeare's mother. She'd hired a limousine to go to the airport and would be arriving any moment now to collect him. Elise raised one hand surreptitiously to her face to wipe the tears away before Shakespeare noticed. He chose exactly that minute to glance up at her.

"You promised you wouldn't cry," he reminded her gently, then reached up himself and dabbed at the corners of her eyes with his own warm hands. "I'll be back here before you know it," he assured her. "Maybe once they get a close look at me they won't even want me and I'll be back here tomorrow in time for Mr. Ouimet to give me a detention."

Elise managed a weak smile. "I doubt it," she said. "I really hope that isn't what happens. I want it to work out well for you, Shakespeare. Really I do."

He shrugged. "I know. But it's a weird business, Elise. Even if I do get the part, there's no guarantee the pilot will sell. I could still end up back here in a couple of weeks, just another high school kid with big dreams.

"I don't want you getting all upset over what might turn out to be nothing at all. And even if things do go well, I'll still be back here as often as I can. I mean, my Mom is here, right? And so is my girlfriend. So it's not as though I'll be gone forever."

Elise nodded as if she agreed with him. But in her heart she couldn't help wondering if he'd ever come back — if she'd ever see him again.

He'd go to Hollywood and get the part in the pilot, and the pilot would become a series and he'd become a star. It'd be his dream come true. Next thing she knew, she'd be watching him on television, then going down to the movie theatre to see him up on the big screen.

He'd be rich and famous and would have girls literally swooning at his feet. Pretty girls. Beautiful girls. Short girls. Girls that were everything she wasn't.

"Let me know how it goes," she said quietly.

"Are you kidding? I'm going to call you the minute I get there. And that's a promise."

She began to smile, but the smile died on her lips. Out of the corner of her eye she saw a streak of black headed their way. The limo.

"Well," said Shakespeare, gazing up at her, "this is it, I guess."

"I'll miss you."

"I love you, Elise." He jumped onto one of the rock markers at the end of the driveway and kissed her. "I'll call you, I promise." Then he ran towards the waiting car.

"Good luck!" she called after him. He turned as he opened the car door and flashed her a smile that melted her heart. Then he was gone, swallowed up by the big black limo as it began to move away from the curb. She watched it until it disappeared around the corner at the end of the street.

Shakespeare didn't call that night after all. Elise convinced herself she hadn't really expected him to. He'd be far too busy. Too many things would be happening. She told herself she was being selfish, thinking only about herself while Shakespeare was facing the biggest break of his life. She told herself it was wrong to even consider the possibility that he might fail at what he was doing. And then, long after the sun had sunk below the horizon, she cried herself to sleep.

She dreamed that someone was calling her name. Only it wasn't Shakespeare; it wasn't a male voice at all. It was a woman's voice. Suddenly an earthquake struck and she was shaking wildly, her whole body rocking back and forth.

"Elise!"

Her eyes flew open. In the shaft of light that filtered in from the hallway, Elise saw her mother's face as she shook her awake. Blearily Elise looked at the clock on the bedside table.

"It's two o'clock in the morning," she said. "Is something wrong?"

"Here, it's two o'clock," her mother said dryly. "In Los Angeles, the night's only just begun. The operator tells me she has a person-to-person call for you from a William Shakespeare Jones in Hollywood. I don't suppose you'd care to take it, would you?"

"Would I?" Elise leapt out of bed and raced out into the hallway to pick up the extension.

"Shakespeare? Is that really you?"

"Yeah, it's me." His voice was so strong, so clear. He could've been standing in the same room. It seemed impossible that he was all the way on the other side of the continent, thousands of kilometres away.

"I've got some good news and some bad news, Elise," he said slowly.

She gulped. She'd been expecting bad news and here it was already.

"What's the good news?" she asked, trying to keep the nervous tremor from her voice.

"The good news is, I'll be home on Saturday."

Her heart soared. Elise felt like she was walking on air. But she forced herself to voice the second question. "And the bad news?"

"The bad news is, I got the part, Elise. Only it's not just for a pilot any more. They've got a firm commitment from one of the networks to pick up the series in the fall."

Elise's lips trembled, but she forced a smile onto them and a happy lilt into her voice as she said, "That's not bad news, Shakespeare. That's terrific news! It's what you've always wanted."

"Yeah, but it means I've got to move out here — at least temporarily. And sooner than I'd expected. And to tell you the truth, Elise, I'm not sure how I feel about that. I mean, it's weird here. People have been making such a fuss over me and I haven't done much yet."

"Not yet," she heard herself saying, "but you will. I know you will."

"My biggest fan, right?"

"Right."

"Can I see you Saturday?"

Could he see her Saturday? Was he kidding?

"Of course you can," she said, laughing into the mouthpiece. "At least, I'm pretty sure I can squeeze you into my busy social calendar."

"Great. Look, I have some dumb press conference to go to when I get there in the morning. Everybody in this business is press crazy like you wouldn't believe. Why don't you hop the bus and meet me downtown in the park around one in the afternoon? We can go somewhere really great for lunch. What do you say?"

She said yes. Immediately.

* * *

Saturday seemed like a year away instead of only a few days. All Elise could think about was how terrific it would be to see Shakespeare again. The thought of being near him almost erased the despair she felt at the inevitability of losing him. Almost, but not quite.

You mustn't think about that, she told herself. You've got to be careful not to ruin everything by being sad and miserable. The important thing is, you're going to see him again.

Besides, she thought, hadn't he said he loved

her? Surely that meant something. If a guy said he loved a girl, shouldn't that give her some hope? Concentrate on that.

The closer Saturday came, the more excited Elise became. She decided she'd make sure she looked sensational this time when they dined out. Well, as sensational as possible.

Finally, Saturday arrived.

"Are you sure you don't want me to drive you?" her mother asked as Elise pulled on a light spring coat over a new dress her father had brought home for her just the day before.

"I thought you were working at home today."

"I am. But if you need a lift..."

"I'll be fine, Mom," Elise said happily. She was so excited, she could've walked the entire twenty-four kilometres into the heart of the city.

She kissed her mother on the cheek and said, "We're going out for lunch, and after that we'll probably hang out in town for a while. I'll call you, okay?"

"Your father and I are going to the art auction later this afternoon, so you won't be able to get us until early evening. And by then I'll expect you to be back anyway." She smiled up at her daughter. "Have a good time, dear."

* * *

Elise boarded the bus at the bottom of the street, and in what seemed like minutes was disembarking at the downtown terminal. She could hardly believe the time had passed so quickly..

She walked to the park to meet Shakespeare.

What a difference from her first visit there with him! Then there had been icy winds blowing snow every which way. Now there wan't a flake of snow to be seen. The grass was still brownish after the winter, but in the beds laid out at regular intervals throughout the park she could see the first small shoots of spring's tulips.

It was sunny enough that Saturday afternoon for shoppers to stop on their way through the park and rest a moment on the benches dotted along the pathways. Almost everyone sitting on the benches was smiling.

It was one of those special first days of spring when people look at each other instead of keeping their heads bowed against the wind and the cold.

Elise wandered through the park, glancing now and again at her watch. It had just turned one. She scouted out an empty bench and sat down. Any moment now she'd look up and see Shakespeare coming her way, fedora perched on his head. She grinned as she savoured that moment.

By two o'clock she was no longer grinning. Instead, she glanced nervously at her watch every minute or two. Where was he? Why didn't he come? Surely press conferences didn't run this long overtime, did they? Her foot tapped impatiently on the pavement as she scanned the streets surrounding the park, looking for his familiar face. Where was he?

At three o'clock she walked to a bank of pay phones at one end of the park. Surely if he'd been detained, he would've called her. He'd never be so cruel as to make her wait the whole afternoon in the park, wondering what had become of him.

The phone on the other end of the line rang and rang. No answer. She counted the rings — twelve, thirteen, fourteen — before she remembered her parents were at the auction.

Even if Shakespeare had been trying to reach them to leave a message for her, he wouldn't have been able to. She dropped the receiver back onto its hook and wiped a tear from her eye. She'd give him another half hour. Well, maybe an hour. But no longer. After that she'd catch the next bus home and just hope that sooner or later he'd call her.

The time that had flown so swiftly in the morning now crept by with dreary slowness. In her heart she knew he wasn't coming, but that didn't stop her from constantly looking around, searching the crowds of faces for that one special face.

All the way home she managed to control her tears. She'd known all along something like this was going to happen. Perhaps not so soon, but it had been inevitable, nonetheless.

It was a little after five when Elise got off the bus at the bottom of her street. She was glad now that her parents weren't home. She'd managed to keep from crying this long, but she didn't think she could keep the tears in much longer.

Elise climbed the front steps and paused to

hunt in her purse for her keys. Suddenly she had to step back as the door flew open.

"Thank goodness!" Her mother exclaimed. "I've been wondering when you'd get back."

Elise forced a smile. "I told you I didn't know when I'd be home," she said as calmly as she could.

"You should've called," her mother said. She looked upset.

"I *did* call, but there was no answer," she said, stepping into the vestibule. "Besides, you said you were going to the art auction." She frowned. "Why *aren't* you there?"

"We were on our way when we heard on the radio. Laura's here."

"You heard on the radio that *Laura's* here?" Elise asked, a confused frown knitting her brow even more.

"No, no," her mother said, shutting the door and steering Elise into the hallway. "Laura's here."

"Mom — "

Elise was about to say that she didn't want to see Laura, but it was too late. As she stepped into the hallway, Laura approached from the sitting room. Elise stiffened. As far as she knew, her mother wasn't aware of the fight between them. She'd just have to try to act naturally. Or as naturally as possible.

"Your father's downstairs," her mother said to Elise, "I'll tell him you're back and he'll drive you."

"Drive me where?" Elise asked, taking her eyes

away from Laura, who looked strangely sad. Or perhaps she was just worried about how Elise would react to her unwanted presence. And just why was she here anyway, Elise wondered. What was going on?

Mrs. Chessman hurried out of the room. Elise looked questioningly at Laura.

"My father was just finishing his rounds," Laura said. "I'd gone to the hospital with him because he was going to drive me into town afterwards. I was supposed to meet Antoine there."

Elise flinched as she heard the name. "How nice," she said carefully. "Well, don't let me keep you."

"Elise — "

"I don't want to hear it, Laura Syms," Elise burst out. "I've had enough. Why don't you just go ahead and meet your boyfriend? I've got to find out what my mother's talking about."

She turned and walked away, abandoning Laura in the living room.

"I know what she's talking about," Laura said, following after Elise.

"Listen to me, Elise." There was an eerie urgency to her voice that stopped Elise cold.

She turned back to Laura.

"I was there at the hospital with my father, sitting in the waiting room," Laura continued. "You know, you've been there before. The big waiting room in emergency where they have the pop machines."

Elise nodded mechanically. Still she wondered

what Laura was babbling about, but something frightening in Laura's eyes kept her from asking.

"There are always ambulances coming and going," Laura continued. "It's no big deal. Half the time when I'm there waiting for Dad I don't even look. It's like if you lived next to a fire station, I guess. After a while you wouldn't think twice about those big trucks racing out in the middle of the night with their sirens wailing."

"Laura, what — "

"I don't know why, but this time when they wheeled in the trolley, I did look, Lord, I couldn't believe it. I tried to call you, but there was no answer. Then I remembered the charity art auction. My mom was on the committee and I know your folks go, so I got hold of Mom — "

"Laura," Elise said stiffly, "I haven't the faintest idea what you're talking about."

At that, Laura began to cry. She pulled a wadded up bit of tissue from her jacket pocket and began to dab at her eyes.

"There was an accident," she mumbled between sobs. "When I left the hospital, they didn't know whether he was going to live or die."

"Laura, *what are you talking about?*" Elise demanded.

"It was Shakespeare, Elise. When I left, my father was about to operate on him."

Chapter 12

Anita Jarvis, Shakespeare's mother, was there, wearing a black hat with a veil that covered her eyes.

Flanking her in the plastic chairs in the waiting room, each holding one of her hands, were two well-dressed men, one in his early thirties, the other much older with grey-flecked hair.

"Those are his agents," Laura explained to Elise, "They were all in the limo together when a truck appeared out of nowhere. The driver of the limo was killed. You know about Shakespeare. They walked away without a scratch."

"What's taking so long?" was all that Elise could say.

Every ten minutes or so, Laura went over to the nurses' station. But she couldn't find out anything, even though she knew half the nurses in the hospital.

"I'm sure Dad will let us know as soon as he can," was the only comfort she could offer.

The evening turned into night.

"Maybe you and Dad should go home," Elise suggested to her mother, who was drinking her tenth cup of coffee. Beside her, her father had fallen asleep, his head resting on Mrs. Chessman's shoulder.

"I'm staying," Mrs. Chessman said grimly. "One way or the other, I'm staying. Just in case…"

She didn't finish the sentence, for which Elise was grateful. She knew what her mother was thinking.

Every now and then, Elise stared over at Anita Jarvis. Her eyes were hidden by her veil so that it was impossible to read anything on her delicate face. But when she wasn't chain-smoking, she was twisting an embroidered linen handkerchief in her hands, so Elise guessed she was as grief-stricken and worried as anyone else in the room.

One of the agents, the younger one, kept going down the hall to one of the pay phones and whispering into the receiver.

"They're probably going nuts wondering what's going to happen to their precious series — " Laura glanced at Elise's face and stopped in mid-sentence. "I'm sorry," she said sincerely.

* * *

Elise was convinced the waiting would drive her crazy. How much longer could she take it? What could be going on?

"Look at it this way," Laura said. "If the news was bad, I'm sure we'd have heard something by now."

Elise had no way of knowing whether this was true or whether Laura was just saying it in an attempt to make her feel better, but she tried to hang on to the thought.

"Would you like another cup of coffee, Mrs. Chessman?" Laura asked.

"Yes, thank you. That'd be nice."

Laura stood up and began to walk down the hall towards the cafeteria on the main floor.

"I'll go with you," Elise offered suddenly as she jumped to her feet and strode after Laura. Laura turned, her face full of surprise.

"It's okay," she said, "I can manage if you'd rather stay here, just in case."

Elise sighed and glanced back at the waiting room. "Your dad will talk to his mother first, anyway. I probably won't even be allowed to see him."

"If it's at all possible, I know Dad will let you in," Laura told her as they walked down the fall. "He always did like you, you know. He must have asked me a million times in the last couple of months how come you don't come around anymore."

Elise nodded. "My mom's been wondering about you too."

The cafeteria was really a small room filled with tables, chairs and banks of vending machines that sold everything from sandwiches to ice cream. Laura dug into her pocket for some change and inserted it into the coffee machine. She glanced speculatively at Elise as she punched the button.

"I guess you're still angry with me, right?" she said at last. "I mean, I did get kind of distracted by Antoine."

Elise sighed. "You did," she said.

Laura nodded as she reached for a plastic lid for the cup. "For what it's worth," she said quietly, "I'm sorry."

"For what it's worth, I know how it could happen," Elise answered her.

"Doesn't make it right though," Laura said.

Elise shook her head. "No, it doesn't."

They began to walk back down the hallway towards the waiting room. "You know," said Laura, "I've missed you. Antoine's a great guy and all, but it's not the same as having a best girlfriend, especially one you've known all your life. I really don't have anyone to talk to anymore. You know, girl talk."

Elise managed a smile. "I know," she said. She took a few more steps before asking, "Is that why you're here? Why you came to tell me?"

Laura nodded. "To tell you the truth, I've been meaning to come over and talk to you for ages now. But I guess I was afraid to. I knew I hadn't exactly treated you the way a friend should. And I guess I was mad at you too. I didn't think you were being fair to me, either."

She glanced uneasily at Elise. "But I guess mostly I was afraid you'd take one look at me and slam the door in my face before I could get a word out."

Elise laughed. "When have I ever slammed a door in your face? Overturning a punch bowl maybe, but door slamming? That's not my style."

Laura stopped a moment. "I don't suppose this could mean we can be friends again?" she said slowly, tentatively.

"I guess it could," said Elise, "if it also means we can forget anything bad ever happened."

Laura's half smile broadened into a wide grin. She threw her arms around Elise, still holding the hot coffee.

"Nice to have you back, friend," she declared.

"Same here," said Elise sadly, returning the hug.

Then out of the corner of her eye she saw Dr. Syms stepping into the waiting room. She froze as he approached Anita Jarvis. Mrs. Jarvis struggled to her feet with the help of the two Hollywood agents. Elise caught her breath, waiting to see what Shakespeare's mother was going to do, what sign she would give about her son's condition.

Dr. Syms took her arm and led her away through some swing doors.

"He'll be back any minute," Laura said as she watched her father disappear. "Then we'll find out."

Side by side, they walked back to the waiting room and handed the coffee to Mrs. Chessman.

"Did you hear anything?" Elise asked her mother anxiously. Mrs. Chessman shook her head. Elise sank down into the next chair and waited.

* * *

It seemed forever before Dr. Syms came back to the waiting room. Laura ran to him, demanding to know how Shakespeare was. The doctor looked pale and weary and Elise found herself whispering a little prayer under her breath. It didn't look good.

"He's critical," Dr. Syms said at last, "and I'm afraid his Hollywood career will be on hold for a few months. But with a lot of rest and care, he should be back to normal before too long."

The air seeped out of Elise in one long, endless sigh. She felt like dancing. He was going to be okay. She rushed to Dr. Syms and flung her arms around him in gratitude.

"He wants to see you, Elise. I'll show you the way."

Elise's heart soared. It was more than she could've dared to hope for. Not only was he going to be fine, but one of his first thoughts had been for her. She started to follow Dr. Syms down the hall, then turned back to Laura.

"Aren't you coming?" she asked.

Laura shook her head. "No. But I'll be waiting for you here, okay?"

"Okay!"